# THE NEW YEAR'S PARTY

CINDY GUNDERSON

# 1

## DECEMBER 31, 1999

"Are you serious?" Karl sighed, setting the plastic bags down in the hallway.

"I'm sorry, I completely forgot about the tarragon," Nicole said, wiping her hands on her apron as she poked her head around the corner from the kitchen. Her chestnut hair was pulled into a messy bun on top of her head, and she apparently hadn't found time to change out of her pajama pants.

"And you can't use anything else?" Karl asked, exasperated.

She shrugged. "That's what the recipe calls for."

"I've been to the store twice already this morning. It's a madhouse."

"I know, I know," she sighed, "I'm sorry I forgot."

Karl took a deep breath, staring forlornly at the groceries on the floor beside him.

Nicole walked into the hall, wrapping her arms around his neck. "I'd like to remind you that this whole thing was your idea."

Karl raised an eyebrow. "No, 'this whole thing' is all you.

My 'whole thing' was more like 'hey, maybe we could invite our friends over and order pizza for New Year's.' Now I'm being sent to the store for blueberry chèvre and—and tarragon."

Nicole laughed lightly, refusing to let him out of her grasp. "I may have gotten a little carried away, I'll admit it. But these are your friends—"

"And your roommates."

"YOU invited them! Plus—"

Karl finally relented and pulled her into a hug. "It's fine; I'm kidding. I'm only *slightly* annoyed that I have to go back out into the freezing cold for the *third* time to buy something I've never heard of."

"It's an herb," she said, her voice muffled against his shoulder.

"I'm sure it is."

Nicole leaned back, Karl's arms remaining tied around her waist. "I promise it'll be worth it."

"Better be," he teased, watching her saunter back to the kitchen. "Do you want me to bring these bags in there?"

"No, I've got it," she called, "Fresh herbs, not dried!"

"Okay, see you in a few."

Karl stepped out the front door of their townhouse and trudged along the walkway he'd shoveled this morning to their car, parked on the street. At least he didn't have to scrape the windshield.

AT FIVE O'CLOCK, THE DOORBELL RANG. NICOLE FRANTICALLY ran up the stairs to finally change her clothes as Karl opened the front door.

"Hey!" Karl grinned, moving aside to let his best friend

in out of the cold. "Nicole!" he called up the stairs, "Evan's here!"

"Be down in a sec!" she yelled back.

"She's changing," Karl explained, turning back to his guests. "And you," he said, nodding toward a woman with dirty blond hair standing next to Evan, "must be Amy."

"Oh, sorry," Evan said, pulling off his winter coat and setting his shoes on the mat. "I should've officially introduced you. This," he motioned toward her with a flourish of his arm, "is Amy."

"Nice to meet you. Here," Karl laughed, holding out his hands. "I've been instructed to put personal belongings in the den."

"Perfect, thanks," Amy said, handing over her wool pea coat. "Brrr!" she said, smiling as she shivered. "It's freezing out there."

"What are you talking about?" Evan scoffed. "This is a perfect Calgary winter day."

"Says someone who's never lived anywhere reasonable," Amy muttered.

Nicole rushed down the stairs just as Karl left the entry and walked through the double doors on his left with coats and purse in hand.

"Hey, Nikki," Evan greeted her warmly, pulling her into a hug. Releasing her, he motioned next to him. "This is my girlfriend, Amy."

"I've heard so much about you," Nicole said, embracing her.

"I'm excited to meet you two finally," Amy said. "It smells amazing in here."

"It must be the tarragon," Nicole commented, catching Karl's eye as he returned to the hallway.

Karl rolled his eyes. "C'mon in, you guys, have a seat. Do you need anything to drink?"

"Just water for me," Amy said, pulling her sweater closed.

"I'll take whatever you're having," Evan added.

As soon as Evan and Amy were settled on the love seat in the living room, the doorbell rang again. Seeing Karl walking down the hall juggling drinks, Evan hopped up to answer it. Nicole began shuttling in hors d'oeuvres from the kitchen as a large group of friends walked in together.

"Where's Mike?" Nicole asked, pulling Karl aside as she set the last of the serving utensils on the buffet against the living room wall.

"No idea," Karl said, looking around the room. "I think everyone else is here, though."

Nicole nodded. "I'm just going to tell them to go for it," she said, motioning to the food. "I don't want it to get cold."

Karl nodded. "He's always late. And you made a ton. I'm sure there'll be plenty of food left when he shows up."

"Isn't he bringing Amanda with him?"

"I think so?"

Nicole shrugged, then pulled him along to greet the newcomers and invite everyone to dig in.

"SORRY I'M LATE," MIKE SAID, LEANING ACROSS THE CENTER console of his Honda Civic. "I should've paged you."

Amanda slid into the passenger seat and kissed him lightly before reaching for her seat belt. "It's okay; I was running behind, too. Kim's got this new laptop she's trying to connect to the internet. Turns out, it takes more than three brunettes and a blond to finish that task."

Mike laughed, pulling away from the curb. "I can take a look at it when we get back."

"Tonight? Isn't this a New Year's party?"

"Yeah," he said slowly, "but I wasn't necessarily planning to stay 'till midnight."

Amanda scoffed. "You're planning to ditch out early on your own brother's New Year's party?"

"Okay," he said in mock defense, "everyone else there is already finished with school or in a Ph.D. program; it's not my normal crowd."

"So you're taking me to a lame party?" Amanda teased.

"No, I'm taking you so *my* party experience *won't* be lame."

"Ah. I see," she grinned, wrapping her hand around his. "So why are we even going to said party if you're not even excited to see anyone there?"

"I didn't say 'anyone.' I'm excited to see my brother and his wife."

"Nicole?"

"Good memory."

"How long have they been married?"

"Almost a year, I think," Mike said, turning on his right blinker.

"Wait, is Alexis going to be there? I guess she's not Nicole's roommate anymore. I still think it's so weird that we have that random connection."

"I honestly don't know," he said. "About the party attendance. She's definitely not her roommate anymore."

"I haven't talked with her in forever."

"Me either."

Mike pulled onto 32nd Ave., and the wheels skidded slightly. He pulled his hand from hers and tightened his grip on the steering wheel.

"Icy?"

"A little. Not too bad. What are you holding?" Mike asked, suddenly noticing the dark package on her lap.

"It's a poinsettia."

"You're holding a live plant?"

"It's a gift," she laughed. "Never show up to a party empty-handed."

"You're a way nicer person than me."

"We can say it's from both of us."

Mike laughed out loud. "Karl's never going to buy that, but I appreciate the offer."

He took the exit to Crowchild Trail, then carefully accelerated. Checking his blind spot, Mike flicked on his signal to merge.

"What's wrong?" Amanda asked, noticing him looking from his side mirror to his rearview three separate times before pulling fully into the right-hand lane.

"I don't know..." he said. "That guy's being sketchy."

"The guy behind you?"

"Yeah. He's weaving in and out of his lane."

"He's probably just messing around," she said, looking in her mirror. "I don't see him."

"He's pulling past us. I think I'm going to slow down and let him get a ways ahead."

"Probably smart."

They watched as a pick-up truck pulled past them on the right, swerving erratically. The truck barreled down the road, barely staying within the lines.

"Not cool," Amanda breathed. "Glad you noticed that."

Mike's body relaxed. "So what are you—"

Before he could finish his sentence, his eyes widened, and he gasped. Amanda's head whipped toward the windshield, but before she could speak, they slammed into the side of the truck that had passed them moments before.

Sounds of shattering glass and crunching metal filled her ears as the car screamed across the icy asphalt. Something hit her head. Hard. Color exploded across her retinas as she began to fall...deeper and deeper into blackness.

THE LIVING ROOM OVERFLOWED WITH LAUGHTER, AND Nicole's eyes sparkled as she absorbed the scene around her. She placed the tray of butter tarts on the buffet, and smiled when Karl caught her attention, motioning for her to join him. She settled into the sofa cushion, straightening her red cocktail dress across her knees.

"No, but get this," Aarov said, gesticulating with his hands. "We hid around the corner coming toward ICT—"

"Wait, back up. I missed the first part," Nicole cut in. "Who was there, and where were you?"

"Karl and I were walking to Bio from the Engineering building."

"In the tunnels?"

"Of course, in the tunnels, you're killing my story, Nic," Aarov teased.

"Sorry, move on. I'm caught up," she laughed.

"So we can hear these girls talking about how scared they are and how creepy it is down there, and Karl pulls me aside and motions for me to be quiet."

"You two should never have been allowed to be roommates," Leena scolded, tossing her long, black hair over her shoulder.

Karl was laughing so hard he couldn't rebut the

comment, and Aarov continued on, completely ignoring his girlfriend's disapproval.

"We waited patiently, and it seriously didn't occur to me until the very last second that this was a terrible idea."

Karl wheezed, "It wasn't until we saw their faces—"

"They absolutely lost their minds," Aarov said, mimicking screaming teenagers, nearly climbing over the back of his chair. "One girl jumped *on* another girl and knocked her to the floor; it was absolute pandemonium."

Nicole couldn't help but laugh, mostly because of Karl's complete lack of composure. Tears were streaming down his face as he watched Aarov reenact their moment of undergraduate terrorism.

"How have I never heard this story?" she gasped, clutching her stomach. "Did you get in trouble?"

"We didn't!" Aarov exclaimed dramatically. "And why, you might ask? Because after this guy," he pointed accusingly at Karl, "who had the idea in the first place, completely ditched me, I did damage control."

Karl keeled over in absolute torment, unable to take a breath.

"He took off back to engineering and left me to deal with the aftermath!" Aarov teased.

"You did not," Nicole laughed, her eyes widening as she looked at Karl. "You left poor, innocent Aarov to console a group of terrified eighteen-year-old girls?"

Karl held up a finger, desperately attempting to catch his breath. When he was finally able to speak, he said, "It's not my fault Aarov didn't run with me."

Aarov sat back in his chair and threw a piece of popcorn at Karl's head. "I sat with them while they cried for at least fifteen minutes."

Leena shook her head, wiping her eyes with a napkin.

"And that's why I'm with you. Because you're so sweet," she said, kissing his cheek.

Karl sighed, pulling the popcorn from his hair. "I'd completely forgotten about that."

"You're lucky I talked them down, or we both could've been kicked out."

"And now look at you!" Nicole said. "Both in stable relationships, renewable energy companies scouting Aarov, Karl getting ready to apply to dental school—"

"Again," Karl said, raising an eyebrow.

"Second time's a charm, isn't that what they say?" Leena teased.

"You're going to get in this time, bro," Aarov said. "Especially with that masters."

Karl nodded and crossed his fingers.

Nicole looked around the room. "Okay, seriously, where is Mike?"

"Is he coming?" Aarov asked.

Karl started toward the phone, but then thought better of it. "I'm guessing he's already on the road."

"I'm getting more food," Leena announced abruptly, standing and picking her plate up off the table. "Everything is so good."

"Thanks," Nicole said absently, watching Karl nervously tap his knee.

"Classic Mike," Aarov said, grinning. "I'm sure he'll show up ten minutes to midnight."

"He's been more responsible lately," Nicole said. "He was even early the other day—"

"Oh, when he came to help me fix the steps in the back," Karl nodded. "Yeah. He was."

"I don't know," Nicole said, taking a sip of her sparkling soda. "You'd think he would've given us a head's up."

"It's fine; I'm sure he decided to hit another party first," Karl joked.

"Should we play that game?" Nicole asked, fishing for a good distraction. "I think everyone's at least gone for round one on the food."

Karl nodded, and Nicole stood, using a spoon to clink against her glass. The room reluctantly fell silent.

"I know we're all having fun chatting, but we have, like, five and a half more hours to kill, so Karl and I came up with some games," she said.

"Strip poker!" Tate called from the corner, and Nicole's old roommate Alexis smacked his arm.

"Ignore my boyfriend," she said, rolling her eyes.

Nicole laughed. "Everyone grab a piece of paper and a pen or pencil from either right there or here on the table," she instructed, pointing to a stack of supplies on the bookshelf across the room. "Your job is to write down the names of ten celebrities. When you're done, rip them into strips like this—" she reached down, picking up two strips of paper she'd made earlier, "and we'll put them in this bowl."

"I'm concerned," Alexis said. "What are we going to have to do with these? You're not making us play charades, are you?"

Nicole raised an eyebrow, grinning. "Ooh, and before we start, has everyone been introduced to each other?"

Heads nodded around the room, but Aarov spoke up. "I haven't met you two yet," he said, pointing to a couple sitting next to Alexis and Tate.

"That's Victoria and Pete," Nicole said. "Victoria, Alexis, and I were all roommates when I met Karl."

"Okay, got it. I'm Aarov; this is Leena. I was Karl's roommate before he met Nicole—right after high school."

"Evan, were you all roommates together?" Alexis asked.

"I was only with you guys for about six months, I think?" Evan answered.

"Right, because then we got that sweet house on Center Street," Karl reminded him.

"Why didn't we stay there? That place was awesome—"

"Okay, reminisce later," Nicole cut in. "Write down your celebrities."

Evan and Karl pretended to be annoyed but followed her instructions. The room was quiet as everyone scribbled their answers on the paper.

"I'm not going first," Victoria murmured, and Pete raised his hand.

"Yes, Pete?" Nicole asked sweetly, playing along.

"Victoria says she wants to go first," he said, dodging her elbow.

Nicole laughed, winking at her friend. "We're going to be in teams. Girls against guys?"

The men in the room roared their approval, which earned them competitive stares, and some light smack-talk from the women in the room.

"Girls get the couch," Nicole said, planting herself firmly back on the cushion next to Karl.

For the first time, she noticed his expression. He had their cordless phone against his ear, and he held up a hand before she could ask what was going on. His face blanched as he nodded and said, "Right, I'll be there as soon as I can."

"Who was that?" Nicole asked, her stomach flipping as he hung up the phone.

"My mom. I have to get to the hospital," he whispered.

"Not Mike..." she breathed, and Karl pursed his lips.

He stood and ran to the entry, pulling his coat off the hook and searching through the pile of boots for his own.

"I'm sorry," he said to the group, rushing out the door.

Evan hastily jumped from his chair, threw on his boots, and ran out after him—not even hesitating to find his coat.

Nicole stared as the door slammed, her heart in her throat and her fingers clamped around her pencil.

"HAVE YOU HEARD ANYTHING?" KARL'S DAD ASKED, WALKING determinedly through the glass doors of the ER toward his son.

Karl shook his head. "I'm not sure if that's bad or good," he shrugged nervously.

"Hi, Evan," Karl's mom said.

"Hey, Deb," Evan said, standing and embracing her. "Ray," he nodded toward Karl's dad. "I'm sorry you had to drive all the way here with it starting to snow like this."

"That was probably the most stressful drive of my life," Ray said as Karl guided him to the open seat next to him. "But not because of the snow."

"Glad you took your time," Karl said, putting an arm around his dad's shoulder. Deb sat next to Evan across from them.

"Did the police tell you anything else when they phoned?" Karl asked softly.

"I'm sure they did, but I couldn't process anything after they said Mike was in an accident," Deb said. "I'm lucky I got the name of the hospital correct."

The double doors to their left opened, and a man in blue scrubs walked through. He searched the waiting room, and when he saw them, walked in their direction.

Deb and Ray stood as he approached.

"McKay family?"

They all nodded.

"I'm Dr. Simon. Would you follow me please?"

Deb looked warily at the men around her, and Karl put his arm around her, ushering her forward. Dr. Simon scanned his card, and they followed him through the doors and down the hall and into a room on the left. As they took their seats on the couches that lined both walls, the doctor shut the door and turned to them.

"As you know, Mike was in a serious car accident earlier this evening—"

"Sorry to interrupt, but could you tell us what happened?" Karl asked, his hands shaking. This room was furnished differently than the waiting room; a landscape painting hung on the wall and there were decorative pillows on the sofa. He suspected this wasn't a place people came to hear their loved one was recovering nicely.

"Of course," Dr. Simon said gently. "Mike was in the car with a young woman named Amanda Reynolds. They were driving west on Crowchild Trail when a Ford F-150 swerved into their lane. There were four individuals in the truck, all of whom are here in the ICU." The doctor paused, glancing at the floor. "The driver's blood-alcohol level was well beyond the legal limit."

"They were hit by a drunk driver," Deb whispered, and the doctor nodded.

"Mike's car rolled once and was found in the ditch. Both Mike and Amanda were unconscious when emergency teams arrived on the scene. It took approximately thirty minutes to remove them from the vehicle. They were transported here by ambulance and both had severe injuries. Mike's left leg was crushed—"

Deb folded in half, her guttural sobs echoing throughout the room. Ray sat stoically next to her, rubbing her back as tears slipped down his cheeks.

"The car crushed his left leg from here down," the doctor continued, sliding his hand along his thigh, just above the knee, "and he experienced massive blood loss. He was given a transfusion prior to arriving at the ER, and two more once he was admitted. He had internal bleeding, facial lacerations, seven broken ribs, his left lung was punctured—"

Karl's ears were ringing. If ever he'd wondered what an out of body experience felt like, this was it.

"—lack of oxygen to the brain—"

He heard the words coming out of the doctor's mouth, but they seemed to float around him, not quite able to penetrate the fog that encompassed his body.

"We did everything we could. The damage to Mike's body was too severe, and we weren't able to save him. He died at 7:02 pm."

Dr. Simon fell silent at delivering this news. Evan placed a hand on Karl's shoulder, and Deb—still pressed against her thighs—was gasping for breath.

"I'll leave you alone for a moment. When you're ready, if you'd press this button," Dr. Simon said, motioning to a red call button on the wall, "a nurse will come in and take you to see Mike. I'm so very sorry for your loss."

With one last glance, the doctor left the room, closing the door softly behind him. The fluorescent lights buzzed, and the ground seemed slightly unsteady as Karl stood. He walked to a counter along the opposite wall, pulled a disposable cup from the dispenser, and then filled it with water from the faucet. The cup shook as he brought it to his lips, forcing himself to take a sip.

His younger brother was dead. He repeated this statement over and over in his mind, attempting to make sense of it. Mike couldn't be dead. He was supposed to come to the party. His pager buzzed in his pocket every few minutes, but he couldn't bring himself to look at the messages. He knew he should call Nicole and let her know what was going on. If there was anything worse than knowing what happened, it was not knowing. But he couldn't do it. Not yet.

"I—I want to see him," Deb stammered, sitting upright. Evan reached over to grab a couple of tissues from the box on the end table. He handed them to her, and she took them gratefully.

"Are you sure you're ready for this?" Karl breathed, tears stinging the corners of his eyes. "It sounded like his injuries—"

Ray held up a hand, a wan smile on his lips. "Press the button," he breathed, and Karl obediently hit it with his palm. A few moments later, a different man in scrubs opened the door and motioned for them to follow him down the hall. As they passed the nurse's station, Karl kept his gaze forward, not wanting to witness the pitying looks that were surely being sent their way.

They followed the nurse into the quietest hospital room he'd ever been in. No beeping or humming equipment, and no movement of hospital personnel. It was somber and stifling.

Mike lay still in the bed, barely recognizable. His face was swollen and bruised, with cuts stretching from his jaw to his forehead. His unruly hair spread across the white pillow, and only his right arm was visible over the sheet and blanket.

Deb collapsed in the chair next to the bed, gripping Mike's arm and sobbing afresh. Ray sat next to her, pulling another chair close and wrapping his hand around hers.

"What happened to her?" Ray called out as the nurse turned to walk from the room.

"Who?" he asked, concern on his face.

"The young woman—Amanda, I think? She was in the car with Mike," Ray said, his words barely audible.

"She's in critical condition."

"Is her family here? We'd like to meet them—"

"We haven't been able to contact her family at this time," the nurse said apologetically.

Deb lifted her head. "She's alone?"

The nurse nodded.

"Can we see her?" she asked.

"Unfortunately, only family is allowed in at this time." He gave a final nod and left the room.

Karl stared at his brother. He needed to find a way to get a hold of Nicole. Maybe the nurse's station had a phone he could use?

"I'm so sorry," Evan said next to him. "I can't believe this."

"Thanks for coming with me," Karl said, and Evan put an arm over his shoulder.


FORTY-FIVE MINUTES LATER, KARL WALKED OUT OF MIKE'S hospital room with Evan and his parents. Somehow, he'd been able to help with paperwork and logistics. He carried a folder with morgue information and myriad flyers for support and mental health resources.

"Is that her?" Evan asked, pointing into the room next to Mike's. The door was slightly ajar, and the top of a folder stuck out of a plastic organizer screwed into the wood. After glancing down the hall to make sure nobody was watching, Evan stepped closer and read the name. Reynolds, Amanda. A petite body lay on the bed, tubes coming out of her arms and a mask on her face. In the low lights, he could barely see her closed eyes and head partially wrapped in gauze.

"I can't believe they haven't been able to contact anyone. She's completely alone. What if she wakes up?" Deb whispered.

"Our friend Alexis knows her. When I phone Nicole, I'll ask if she has some connection the police aren't aware of," Karl said. "But I wouldn't worry about her waking up. I'm sure she's on a lot of morphine."

"But haven't you heard of those studies? That people live longer when someone is there to hold their hand and talk with them?" Deb continued. "If she's in critical condition—"

"I'll go sit with her," Karl offered. "What's the worst that could happen, they kick me out?"

Deb smiled at him gratefully. "If this girl was important to Mike, I just don't feel good about leaving her alone."

"Karl, you need to get back to Nicole. And the next few days are going to be rough. Let me stay," Evan offered. "You need more sleep than I do."

"I doubt I'll be able to sleep," Karl said.

"But you need to be with your family, and with Nicole."

Karl nodded. "Don't get arrested," he said with as much humor as he could muster, clapping him on the back.

"You'll bail me out, right?" Evan hugged Deb and Ray, then walked into the dimly lit room and took a seat.

AN HOUR OR SO LATER, EVAN BLINKED AWAKE WHEN A NURSE walked into the room. Her eyes widened when she saw him seated next to the bed.

"Who are you?" she asked, holding Amanda's chart in one hand and placing the other on her hip.

"I'm—a family member," he said, less confidently than he would've liked.

"Now I know that's not true," she scolded, setting down her clipboard and walking to the head of the bed. "We haven't been able to get a hold of any of her family."

"What if I got the message and came right over?"

"Then I would've been informed. And I was *not* informed," the nurse said, lifting the gauze and flashing him a look.

Evan sighed. "I'm Mike's brother." He figured that was almost true. Mike and Karl were the closest things to brothers he'd ever had. "He died tonight and Amanda was in the car with him. We didn't want her to be alone."

"We?"

"His—my family."

"So you snuck in here to sit with her?"

Evan nodded.

"Her actual family might get here at any moment."

"But then you'd be informed. And you could inform me," Evan said, the corner of his mouth lifting.

The nurse rolled her eyes. "If I don't kick you out of here, I could get in a lot of trouble."

"Only if I cause a problem. And I promise I won't. Have you heard about the studies that say patients have a better survival rate when—"

"I know the studies," she said sternly, "but as far as I can tell, you're just sitting there."

Evan opened his mouth to speak, but nothing came out.

"Hold her hand for goodness' sake. Do you sing?"

Evan shook his head.

"You better start then," she said, walking into the hall and bringing in a new bag of fluids. She took the nearly empty bag from the pole and replaced it, then connected it to the IV tube. "I did not see any of this," she said, picking up the clipboard and making a note. "All I know is this girl is going to be touch-and-go all night. She needs all the help she can get."

Evan watched the nurse stalk back out into the hall. He looked at the pale hand on the blanket in front of him. Gingerly, he reached out and lifted it into his own, surprised at how cold it was. Her finger flinched, and he jumped, his heart pounding. Was it just him, or was the machine monitoring her heart rate beeping faster?

He rubbed her hand between his, hoping the friction would warm it up a touch. The nurse had told him to sing, but he hadn't sung anything since high school. And that had been a Queen parody for Grad. Not really calm and comforting material. He wracked his brain for something he could talk about.

"Hey Amanda, my name's Evan," he said hesitantly. "I'm Mike's friend. You guys had a rough night, and it's New Year's Eve, so that...really sucks. But let's not talk about stuff that sucks, okay?"

He shook his head, finding it more difficult than he thought to talk to someone who couldn't respond.

"I'm going to tell you a story," he said, forcing a smile. "You may have heard it before, but it's the only one I can think of right now. So, there's this guy who wanted to be a professional hockey player. He had a fantastic slap shot, but wasn't great at stick handling or skating—kind of essential skills—so he wasn't making much progress.

"Then one day, he showed up at his grandmother's house to find out she was being forced to move—she hadn't paid her taxes in years. And, I forgot to mention, his grandma was kind of his only real relationship, so he wanted to help her. Sorry, I'm not very good at this," he said, glancing at the door to make sure nobody was watching.

"Anyway, he shows up to her house and finds workers using his grandpa's old clubs to hit golf balls, and he ends up betting them—I can't remember exactly why at first, but then he bets them for money and wins. That gives him the idea that he could earn money to repurchase his grandma's house—"

Suddenly, he heard his name drifting into the room from the speakers in the hall. Was his brain playing tricks on him? He jumped from his seat and listened. And yes, he was definitely being paged to the nurses station.

Taking a deep breath, he walked down the hall. When he approached the desk, the nurse he'd just met was holding up a phone in one hand with her other hand on her hip.

"Make it fast," she said quietly, then turned and walked into the back.

"Hello?"

"Evan, are you alright?" Amy's concerned voice sounded on the other end of the line.

"Hey, Amy," he sighed.

"Are you still at the hospital?" she asked. "Karl said you were staying with the girl who was in his brother's car."

"Yeah, I'm still here."

"None of her family has shown up?"

"Not yet," he said, checking the clock. "Wow, it's already eleven?"

Amy exhaled. "I was kind of hoping..."

"Amy—"

"I know, it's stupid. With everything that happened tonight, I shouldn't be thinking about my own New Year's experience," she muttered.

"Is everyone still there?"

"Yes. Karl got back, and everyone offered to leave and give them some space—Alexis said she would take me home—"

"That's right, I drove—"

"No, it's not a big deal. But Karl and Nicole both said they'd rather everyone stay. I just feel a little awkward...I don't know any of them well..."

"Amy, I'm so sorry. I offered to stay so Karl could go home, but I didn't think about the fact that you'd be on your own with people you just met."

Amy was silent for a moment. "I feel so bad for them," she whispered.

Evan nodded.

"I'm so sorry, Evan."

Tears sprung to his eyes, and his head lolled in utter exhaustion.

"Are you going to stay all night?" she asked. "It's fine either way; I just think I'll probably take someone up on a ride home if so."

He took a deep breath. "I told Karl's mom I'd stay with her. I have no idea how long that'll be."

"Okay. Maybe we can talk tomorrow?"

"I'll send you updates when I know—"

"Happy New Year, Evan."

"You too," he said as the call ended. He couldn't tell if she'd sounded more tired or upset. They'd been dating for almost a month, but they'd never had to work around something this intense.

Reaching over the counter, he replaced the phone in the dock, then silently slipped back down the hall. Closing the door, he again took a seat next to the bed and breathed a sigh of relief.

Evan looked back at the still, blanketed body in front of him. The machine across from him beeped in a regular rhythm, and the oxygen mask's high-pitched whistle had become background noise for him at this point.

"That was my girlfriend phoning me," he said softly. "Kind of a new relationship. We met at my friend's Thanksgiving dinner in Okotoks. It took me almost three weeks to get up the courage to ask her out." He chuckled, remembering how nervous he'd been to dial her number.

"Back to the story," he whispered. "So, this guy figures out he can make a lot of money betting people on his golf swing, and then—"

He stopped, looking down at his hand. Amanda's fingers were moving. She squeezed his hand, and her leg shifted under the blanket. Evan looked up and saw her eyelids flicker. His heart hammered in his chest. What was she going to think when she saw a complete stranger sitting next to her hospital bed?

Her eyes opened—blinking rapidly at first, but then her gaze locked onto his. They stared at each other, and Evan's voice caught in his throat. Slowly, her eyelids drooped, and she relaxed into her pillow once again, her hand falling still.

Evan took a deep breath. She didn't freak out. That was a good sign, right? Relieved, he pulled his chair closer and lay his head on his left arm, resting on the empty strip of mattress next to where his right hand continued to grip hers.

"He ends up joining a golf tournament to try and win the money," he continued, yawning. "The other golfers hate him because he's nothing like them, but he kind of becomes a hero...and meets this guy who lost a hand to an alligator. Sounds weird, but it's pretty funny..."

Evan's words began to slur as he closed his eyes. His

breathing slowed, and eventually, he fell asleep to the sound of beeping, whistling, and humming.

"TEN MINUTES TO MIDNIGHT," ALEXIS SAID SOFTLY. SIX OF them—Alexis, Victoria, Aarov and Leena, and Karl and Nicole—sat in a tight circle in the living room. Pete, Tate, and Amy had all gone home shortly after Amy's phone call with Evan.

"Thanks for staying, guys," Nicole breathed.

Karl nodded. "I'm sorry this is kind of the worst New Year's Party ever."

"We all knew and loved Mike," Aarov said, putting a hand on Karl's shoulder. "We wouldn't want to be anywhere else. Plus, if Y2K's a thing, I wouldn't want to be with anyone else when the world ends."

"Thanks for that," Alexis said, a smile threatening to erase her solemn expression.

"Have you heard from Evan?" Nicole asked.

"No," Karl shook his head. "I'm sure he'll get in touch when he leaves," Karl said, hunching over and resting his arms on his thighs. "I can't believe Mike's gone. It's so strange. I just saw my brother's body lying in a hospital bed, and then...I drove home. And he doesn't exist anymore."

"And now we're starting a new year without him," Nicole said, her voice catching.

Alexis wrapped an arm around Nicole's shoulder and pulled her close. "I feel like I should be there at the hospital with Amanda."

"I gave them the info you had," Karl said. "I highly doubt they'd let you back there even if you did go over."

"I know," Alexis breathed, still holding tightly to her

friend. "And Nicole, Mike would've loved this party. Butter tarts were his favorite."

"And shrimp," Victoria grinned, "Remember when he ate shrimp out of my noodle bowl that year we went out for Karl's birthday?"

"He was the worst!" Leena laughed. "He stole a bite of my cake that year, too!"

Karl laughed. "He would've loved everything about this party." Sitting up, he looked around the room. "We've been friends for almost eight years now."

"Over eight," Victoria said, smiling softly.

"I know our lives are probably going to take different paths in the next year or two, but...what if we did this again," Karl said.

"Did this?" Leena asked.

"Like a New Year's party. To celebrate Mike. What if we did this every year, no matter where we are or what we're doing. We could meet wherever."

Nicole wiped a tear from her cheek. "I'm automatically in," she grinned.

"We're in," Aarov said, and Leena reached for his hand. "And I'll speak for Evan."

"Of course we're in," Alexis and Victoria both nodded.

"Two minutes," Leena said, watching her clock. "This year, my goal is to appreciate the people I love."

"I don't want to take anything for granted," Alexis said, her cheeks flushed with emotion.

"I want to be more fun," Karl said, wrapping his arms around Nicole.

"You're going to have to work hard at that, eh?" Aarov said, nudging Karl with his elbow. "I want to be less fun. Because I'm too fun already, and Leena says I need to take things more seriously."

Leena laughed. "You know those engineers. So fun."

Aarov scoffed, feigning offense.

"Ten, nine, eight—" Leena started the countdown, and everyone joined in.

"Happy New Year," they said together, standing and embracing each other.

As Karl pulled Nicole away from her roommates, he held her tightly in his arms. He knew in a few minutes, this room would be empty besides the two of them, and they'd have to walk upstairs and go to bed. And wake up tomorrow in a world without Mike.

## 2

# DECEMBER 31, 2000

Amanda paced across the kitchen floor. She'd been avoiding the fact that this day was coming for weeks now, but it did nothing to help the onslaught of emotions waiting for her when she woke up this morning.

One year. It had been one year since their accident. And she'd been invited to attend the same party she was supposed to attend last year with Mike. At least this time, she actually knew the people who would be there, but the reason she knew them...

Was it possible to have a positive experience with people linked to trauma?

Amanda squeezed her eyes shut and leaned against the counter. She didn't have to go. She could curl up in her bed right now and watch movies the rest of the day, or go out with her roommates to a raging New Year's Eve bash and numb herself for a few hours.

Taking a deep breath, she turned and opened the fridge. She needed to eat something.

"Looking fancy," Jera teased, walking into the kitchen in faux leather pants and a blue metallic tank top.

Amanda turned, looking her up and down. "It's ten-thirty in the morning. It's a lot more normal for me to be in my pajamas than for you to be in...that."

Jera laughed, reaching for a glass in the cupboard next to the sink. "How did *I* get a roommate who is such a homebody?"

"I'm not a homebody," she said, pulling out a jug of milk and a Tupperware with boiled eggs, setting both on the counter.

"Then why aren't you coming with us today?"

"You know why." Amanda waited for Jera to move, then opened the cupboard next to her and retrieved a plate and bowl.

"But you said you didn't even want to go to that party," Jera argued, filling her glass with milk and sitting down at the small, round table. Her short hair and ear gauges typically made her look intense, but this morning—despite the outfit—her make-up-less face looked almost wholesome.

Amanda poured a bowl of Shreddies and set an egg on her plate, then rummaged for a spoon in the silverware drawer. She carried everything to the table and sat down across from her roommate.

Amanda sighed. "I don't know. I feel a lack of motivation to do pretty much anything right now," she said, taking a bite.

"Like I said, homebody."

"No, I don't even want to be *here*," she said, her mouth full of cereal. "Even when I sleep, I wake up with pressure behind my eyes and a mild headache. In quiet moments, all I hear is crunching metal, and I swear I can smell gasoline. And I see Mike—"

"I thought all of that got better in the spring?"

"Yeah, well, it's recently gotten a lot worse."

Jera tapped her glass. "Makes sense, considering the timing of it. Are you feeling anxious about driving again?"

Amanda nodded, reaching for the salt and pepper.

"Why didn't you say something?"

Sprinkling her eggs, Amanda shrugged. "I thought it would go away."

"Are you still meeting with that therapist?"

"I haven't been. But maybe I need to again."

Jera smiled pityingly. "Don't you think getting out would be a good thing? Like, getting in a car on New Year's and going to a party with your favorite roommate and *not* having an accident—wouldn't that kind of rewire your brain or something? Put a good memory in there to outweigh the bad one?"

"I don't think it works like that."

"How would you know?" Jera teased, raising an eyebrow.

Amanda laughed, attempting to keep chewed egg from spilling past her lips. "If I go anywhere tonight, I think it has to be Nicole's party. They're doing a memorial for Mike, and I kind of do want to be there."

Jera nodded. "There's no ice on the roads, surprisingly. That helps, right?"

"It wasn't the ice that killed Mike."

Jera's expression sobered as she stood and put her empty glass in the sink. "Do you miss him?" she asked softly.

"How could I not?"

Jera squeezed her shoulder as they passed, walking toward the front door. "Well, if you get bored, we're going to be setting up at Outlaws. Dinner's catered again this year, and you know when the doors open, it's going to get nuts."

"Thanks," Amanda smiled. "Be safe."

Taking her time, Amanda finished her breakfast and

rinsed her dishes. Walking back to her room, she lay down on her bed and pulled up the covers.

*"Hey, Amanda, right?"*

*"Yeah," she said slowly. "Are you in my Stats class? I'm sorry, I don't remember your name."*

*"Mike," he said, holding out a hand. "I'm in Stats and Ethics."*

*"Really?" Amanda said, taken aback. "That's not a huge class, and I've never seen you in there."*

*"I said I was in it, not that I attended," he said, obviously amused with himself.*

*"Ah," Amanda said, picking up her books from the study hall table. "So you're one of those? Handsome 'cool guy' who thinks he's above having to attend class."*

*"You think I'm handsome?"*

*Amanda rolled her eyes, walking past him toward the exit.*

*"Skip class tomorrow."*

*She spun around to face him. "Why would I skip class tomorrow? Unlike you, I have plans that require me not failing out of undergrad."*

*"Just once. I'll even help you catch up on what you missed. Call it an act of service."*

*"For who, you?"*

*Mike nodded, grinning. "I feel very misjudged right now, and I'd like to show you something tomorrow morning. Skipping one eight o'clock class isn't going to kill your grade."*

*She stood there, tapping her foot. "If you think I'm going to go anywhere with you alone, you're crazy."*

*"So bring a friend, I don't mind."*

*"What time?"*

*"Meet me at the zoo. North entrance. Five-thirty."*

*Amanda looked at him quizzically. "In the morning?"*

*Mike nodded.*

*"The zoo? You're not going to murder us..."*

*"Promise."*

*Amanda nodded nervously, then turned and walked briskly through the double doors.*

"How's it looking?" Nicole asked, poking her head out onto the patio.

"I think the temperature is pretty stable, surprisingly," Karl said. "I wondered if I was going to need to add a bunch more wood chips with it being so cold."

He stood up and walked back inside, rubbing his hands together. "Next year, I think I'll smoke stuff when there's a chinook and then put it in the freezer."

Nicole laughed. "That would mean we'd need an actual freezer."

"Which would mean we'd need a bigger place," Karl said, putting his cold hands under the back of her shirt.

She shrieked, pushing him away. "I guess we can discuss that when we know details."

"I know, I know," he sighed, walking toward the fridge. "Want me to chop the veggies for you?"

"Always."

"No last-minute trips to the store?"

Nicole rolled her eyes. "Are your parents coming?"

"I don't think so," he said, pulling out the cucumbers, two red peppers, and a bag of carrots. "They felt like tonight could be friends, and we'll do our family thing tomorrow." He set the veggies next to the sink.

"Has Amanda gotten back to you?"

Karl shook his head. "I hope she comes. I'm worried about her."

"Why?" Nicole asked, pulling out her mixer to make the filling for the butter tarts.

"I don't know. I think it's weird she hasn't re-enrolled. And she hasn't been responding to me lately."

"Email?"

Karl nodded, taking a peeler out of the drawer and working on the carrots.

"Maybe she's been busy with Christmas. I don't think it's odd for her to take a year off school."

"But it's her last semester. She could be finished and not have to work at that restaurant anymore."

Nicole shrugged. "It probably feels a little overwhelming."

"I know, but after a year?"

When Nicole didn't answer, he turned his head. "What?" he asked, seeing her arms folded across her chest.

"We're all still grieving, Karl. You just happen to grieve by throwing yourself headlong into new projects, but for some people? It feels better to pull back."

He turned around to the sink. "Just seems like that would make it worse," he said softly.

Nicole walked forward and pressed herself against his back, wrapping her arms around him.

"So you're the one crazy enough to marry my brother?" *Mike asked with a wide grin.*

*"Seems that way," Nicole smiled, reaching out a hand.*

*Mike ignored it and threw his arms around her. Pulling back, he smiled. "So. Tell me about yourself."*

"Ummm," Nicole hesitated, looking nervously at Karl, who stood next to her. "I just graduated with a degree in—"

"No," Mike cut in. "Tell me about you. What matters most to you in the world? What scares you?"

"Sorry," Karl shrugged, with an amused look on his face. "I warned you."

Nicole chewed on her lower lip. "Family matters most to me in the world," she said softly. "My dad died when I was little, and my mom hasn't ever been the same since. So, I haven't had that close-knit family that I hear people talk about. I want one."

Mike smiled encouragingly, waiting for her to go on.

"What scares me? Losing someone I love. I didn't get to feel that when my dad died, and everything I feel now is so horrible that I can only assume dealing with that in the moment must be a million times worse. That terrifies me."

Mike put a hand on Karl's shoulder. "I think we can help you with the family part."

"GIRRRL, YOU NEED TO HURRY! WE HAVE TO PICK UP TATE ON the way," Alexis called down the hall, rushing to the coat closet. "Who are you getting ready for anyway? You know no single guys are going to be there."

"Thanks for that," Victoria said, meeting her in the living room. "It's still New Year's Eve, and I want to look nice."

Alexis took in her black pencil skirt and shimmery blouse. "You look great. Now can we please get in the car?"

Victoria adjusted her glasses and looked in the mirror next to the door. "Do you think I should do something with my hair?" She ran her hands through her shoulder-length bob.

"It's pretty down."

"Are you just saying that because you want to leave?"

"I guess you'll never know," Alexis said, throwing a coat into her arms and motioning toward the shoe bin.

Victoria rolled her eyes but slipped into her coat and put on her black ankle boots. "Are we picking Tate up at home?"

"No, he's barely getting off work. We'll grab him on the way to Karl and Nicole's. Want me to drive?"

"Sure," Victoria nodded, tossing her the keys.

The girls stepped onto the front walkway, and Alexis locked the door behind them. They hopped into Victoria's Rav4 and turned on the engine, letting it warm up for a second before pulling onto the street.

"Are you nervous about tonight?" Victoria asked quietly.

"Why?"

"Just because...I don't know how Karl and Evan are going to be. And I always feel so awkward talking to people who've lost someone. I never know the right thing to say."

"I mean, it's been a year. I'm not saying they're suddenly over it, but they're definitely more normal. Remember how they all were right after it happened compared to last month when we got together?"

Victoria nodded.

"It didn't even feel like they were the same people then. That's not a criticism; it's just true," Alexis finished. She held onto the arm rest as Victoria turned sharply to the right.

"No, I know. I remember wondering if Nicole was ever going to have fun again. It was like she didn't want to laugh in case Karl happened to be around," Victoria said.

"Death is just...weird. And hard."

"I didn't have as much of a relationship with Mike as you did, but I still miss him. When we got together for Nicole's birthday in the summer? That's when I really noticed his absence. It was like there was a hole that nobody else could fill."

Alexis exhaled loudly. "I know, I felt it too."

"Remember that year he walked into the restaurant dressed like a Chippendale dancer?"

"Ummm, yes!" Alexis laughed out loud. "Remember Nicole's face?"

"And when he stood on the chair seductively eating fries off her plate?"

"What ended up happening? Did he get kicked out?"

"No, Evan brought him clothes in his backpack; remember the manager came over, and he quickly dressed?"

Alexis snorted, attempting to focus on the road ahead of her as her friend laughed hysterically next to her.

"There's Tate," Victoria pointed to the front of the parking lot they'd just pulled into, wiping tears from her cheeks. "Want me to get in the back?"

"No way, he can sit back there," Alexis said, pulling up to the curb and unlocking the doors.

Rolling down the passenger side window, Alexis leaned over and gave him a smoldering look. "Hey gorgeous, are you for hire?"

Tate grinned and walked to her side of the vehicle, insisting she roll down her window so he could kiss her before jumping in the back seat.

"Ladies, how's your last day of the year two-thousand going?" Tate asked.

"Incredible now," Alexis grinned, pulling slowly through the lot. "And pumped that we don't have to worry about the world ending this New Year's."

"Y2K. What a joke," Tate laughed. "I'm excited to hang out tonight. And eat more of Nicole's food. Do you think she's making the same stuff?"

"Oh, crap!" Alexis said, slamming on the brakes. "I forgot. We were supposed to bring drinks."

Victoria looked at her in surprise. "Since when?"

"I forgot to tell you. I offered to bring something the other day when I was helping Nicole paint."

"So *you* were supposed to bring drinks," Victoria teased.

"There's a liquor store over—" Tate started, but Alexis held up a hand.

"Nope. Karl's given strict instructions. No alcohol."

Tate stared at her in stunned silence. "But it's a New Year's Party."

"Dude," she said, turning fully in her seat. "His brother was killed by a drunk driver. Are you saying you can't have fun without alcohol for a night?"

Before Tate could respond, a car honked behind them.

"Alright, alright! I'm going. Is there a Co-op around here?" Alexis asked, putting the car in gear.

"Turn right, and then I think there's one a couple of blocks up," Victoria offered. "What if we did French sodas?"

"What are those?" Tate asked.

"It's like soda water, those flavorings that come in those glass bottles, you know?" she explained, miming with her hands. "Then you add milk. They're delicious."

"Done," Alexis said. "Do you think Nicole will have ice?"

"Hmmm...not sure..."

"I see the Co-op. Tate, go grab a bag of ice just in case. We'll get the other stuff. Divide and conquer!"

Tate groaned, but didn't argue as Alexis pulled into a parking space.

"Meet back here in ten!"

"But what if I'm faster than that? I don't want to stand out here in the cold," Tate complained, and Alexis tossed him the keys as she grabbed Victoria's hand and ran into the store.

"YOU REALIZE YOU OWE ME BIG TIME FOR THIS," ALEXIS YAWNED. "Who in their right mind gets up at five A.M. on a Thursday?"

"I think a lot of normal adults get up this early for work," Amanda said.

"Yeah, but we're not normal people. We don't have to do crap like this for another year or two, and I'd like to take advantage of that fact fully."

"I definitely owe you big time—A-for the use of your car, and B-for coming with me so I don't get chopped up into little pieces and fed to the tigers."

"Is this dude a total weirdo?"

Amanda shook her head. "I don't think so? There's something about him. It could either be that he's incredibly cool...or that he's a psychopath."

"I mean, I'll take those odds," Alexis laughed, taking a Timbit out of the box that sat between them on the console. "And you owe me coffee for the rest of the week."

"Done," Amanda smiled.

They pulled into the zoo entrance, and Alexis slowed down. "Where do you think we should park?"

"There!" Amanda exclaimed, pointing to a man waving them down near the front. He guided them into a "Zoo staff only" parking spot.

"If I get a ticket..." Alexis said under her breath, but then noticed the official zoo uniform he was wearing. "Wait, is that Mike?"

"Yeah," Amanda nodded. "Wait, how do you know his name?" She looked at her friend in confusion.

"My roommate Nicole is dating his older brother," Alexis said. "How did you meet him?

"He's in one—I guess two—of my classes," she said, slinging her purse over her shoulder and stepping out of the car.

Alexis pulled on her leather jacket—grabbed the box of Timbits—and followed her.

"Okay," Amanda said, "We're here."

"Hey," he smiled, then turned to Alexis. "Oh, hey," he said slowly. "Alexis, right?"

"Yeah," she said, still obviously weirded out by the connection. "You two are friends?" he asked.

Amanda nodded. "We used to work at the same restaurant."

Mike nodded. "Small world. We're going this way," he said, opening a utility door and ushering them into a plain hallway.

They walked behind him, their footsteps echoing against the painted brick walls.

"Turn here," he said, and they followed him through another door back onto the main zoo path.

"It's so weird being here when it's empty like this," Amanda said.

"I think it's peaceful," Mike said. "All the animals are waking up, the plants are coming alive. That's why I do this."

"And what is 'this' exactly..." Alexis asked.

"I'm a volunteer zookeeper," he said, spinning around to walk backward.

Amanda's eyes widened. "Seriously?"

"Yep. I've been working here since I was in high school, and last summer, I did a certification that allows me to actually work with the animals."

"And you don't get paid?" Alexis asked.

"Oh, I get paid. Just not in cash. You'll see," he said, turning forward with a massive smile on his face. How much did she really know about Karl's younger brother? She'd seen him at the *apartment a few times, but she fully understood Amanda's description at this point. And she really hoped he wasn't a psychopath.*

*He led them through another side door and down a hallway like the first. This time, he led them into a room full of boxes and cages, with walls completely covered in glass cabinets.*

*Mike walked to one side, opened a door, and pulled out what looked like a massive baby bottle. The girls watched as he mixed a vial of white liquid into the bottle, added two scoops of powder from a canister, and then poured half hot water, half cold until the mixture reached the top.*

*"This way," he said, shaking the bottle and leading them back out into the hall.*

*Amanda and Alexis walked in silence.*

*"Here we are," Mike said, unlocking a door and stepping into the early morning sunlight. "Watch your step."*

*Alexis walked in first and scanned the small space. It was an enclosure, or at least part of it.*

*"What's in here?" Amanda asked nervously.*

*Mike hushed them as he opened the gate. "She was found injured. We're trying to get her back up to weight."*

*Alexis watched as Mike tapped on the metal and gently clicked his tongue. Two golden paws stretched out from a crate in the corner. Slowly, what looked like a huge kitten walked lazily toward them.*

*"Is that a lion?" Alexis asked.*

*"Mountain lion," Mike said, smiling. "C'mon, I've got your breakfast," he called sweetly.*

*"Was that formula you mixed in the bottle?" Amanda asked.*

*Mike nodded, still watching the cat. "Antibiotics and infant formula. She had a pretty intense laceration along her left leg when they brought her in."*

*The cat reached the door and looked warily at them. They*

stood still while Mike reached out and petted the kitten's head. She quickly warmed up, and he sat down, letting her climb into his lap. He slipped the bottle into her mouth and she immediately began to purr.

Amanda giggled next to her. "Do you hear that?"

"It's like an engine," Alexis said in awe.

"Do you want to pet her?" Mike asked.

The girls nodded emphatically and slowly moved closer.

"Turns out, you're not a murderer," Amanda said.

"Not yet, anyway," Mike teased.

Alexis reached out and touched the soft fur of the kitten's neck. "I'm touching a mountain lion right now," she breathed.

Mike grinned. "Pretty cool, right?"

Alexis nodded, her mind abuzz. She needed more payouts like this in her life.

EVAN STARED AT HIMSELF IN HIS NEW BATHROOM MIRROR. Wiping the steam from the glass, he checked to make sure he'd gotten all the green flecks from between his teeth when he brushed. Dill pickle chips, man. He'd never eat those right before an outing again.

Walking into his bedroom, he pulled on a clean, button-up shirt and khakis. It wasn't particularly dressy, but it would pass. He was more in the mood to be comfortable tonight, and he knew Karl wouldn't care. Nicole was the one who wanted everything to be fancy. Amy certainly didn't mind the excuse to dress up. What was it with women and special occasions?

Walking back into the bathroom, he pulled a bit of pomade from a jar and worked it into his hair. Not bad. Retracing his steps, he pulled his car keys from the desk next to his bed and his coat from the oversized chair in the corner. He'd lived on his own for almost six months now but still hadn't gotten out of the habit of keeping everything in his bedroom. One of these days, he'd actually use the coat closet.

Opening the garage, he slid into the driver's seat of his Honda Accord and pulled out to the street.

Amy was watching for him, and the second he pulled into her driveway, she opened the door and walked carefully down the front steps. As he'd predicted, she was decked out. High-heels and all.

"Hey," she said, a burst of cold air rushing into the car as she sat in the passenger seat.

"You look beautiful," Evan said, smiling at her. "What's that?" He motioned to a platter she was holding, covered in tin foil.

"I made peppermint fudge and thought I'd share," she smiled, looking quite pleased with herself.

Evan reached his hand toward the edge of the foil, but she smacked it away.

"Wait for the party!" she laughed.

The drive to Karl's place took only ten minutes, which meant they arrived earlier than expected. Evan parked his car, realizing as he pulled in that this was the same spot as last year. He hesitated before turning off the engine.

"You okay?" Amy asked.

"I think so?" he answered, taking a deep breath. "I've been fine all day, but right now—pulling up and parking here—" he stopped short. They sat in silence a moment, and Evan stared out the windshield, attempting to calm his racing heart.

"D'you know what I tell my students?" Amy said, unbuckling her seatbelt and turning toward him. "There are so many kids in middle school who have test anxiety, and I know it's far from the same thing, but I think it might help. They spend all this time trying to push away worries that feel mild, and then all of a sudden—when they hit the right trigger—it becomes overwhelming."

Evan nodded.

"I've found it's helpful to take a minute to feel it. To let it all come up—to stop fighting so hard. And then it passes, and the anxiety lessens."

"I don't think I've been pushing it away..." Evan said, his hands still on the wheel.

Amy shrugged. "If you dig a little, what are you feeling right now?"

"It's like—kind of a sick feeling."

"Are you trying to get rid of it?"

Evan looked over, unsure. "Maybe? I want it to go away so we can have a good time."

"Okay, perfect. So what if you just let it go free and wash over you?"

"Then I'd probably throw up," he chuckled.

"Try it."

Evan rested his head on his hands and tried to relax. As he did so, the sickness and dread within him grew. He felt awful. Unease seemed to spread through his entire body—darkness traveling through his limbs and into his fingertips and toes. Moments from the party last year flashed through his mind. Running after Karl in the snow, driving behind him on slick roads, sitting in the hospital waiting room—he shuddered, remembering Karl's parent's faces when they heard the news...

He squeezed his eyes closed as tears collected and his face flushed with heat, reminding himself to breathe.

"YOU GUYS ARE OLD!" MIKE CALLED TO THEM FROM THE TOP OF *the cliff. "You've lost your sense of wonder!"*

*"Not wanting to die isn't a lack of wonder!" Evan yelled back. "That's got to be what, forty feet?"*

*"You've already done twenty; what's a few more?" Mike taunted. He gave a primal yell and launched himself off the cliff.*

*When he surfaced from the churning, deep blue water, he whipped his hair out of his eyes and swam toward them.*

*"Your turn!" he taunted. "Are you going to let an eighteen-year-old kid out-jump you?"*

*Evan shook his head and headed toward the bank.*

SUCKING IN A BREATH, EVAN MARVELED AT THE SCENE THAT had popped into his brain. He hadn't thought about that day in...probably years? The nausea began to retreat, and his muscles relaxed. He lifted his head and looked at Amy, his eyes wide.

"Crazy, right?" she grinned. Reaching out, she gently placed her hand on the side of his face. "I know tonight's going to be hard, but I'm here to make it better. I'll be right there next to you, okay?"

Evan nodded, brushed his lips against her wrist, and opened his door.

KARL AND NICOLE'S LIVING ROOM LOOKED DIFFERENT THAN when he'd last seen it. New couches, hard-wood flooring, and he was almost positive the walls were a different color.

"It looks great in here," Amy commented, "When did you two do all this? We were here two months ago!"

Nicole beamed. "We got so lucky. Our landlord wanted to make some updates, so he *paid* us to put in the flooring and paint!"

"And you didn't phone me to help?" Evan said, feigning offense.

"If we had to do more than three-hundred square feet, I would've reached out, I promise," Karl laughed. "He paid for someone to rip out the carpet, and the flooring was super easy to install."

"That's not what he said when we got to that corner," Nicole said under her breath, pointing to the entryway.

"Well, the wall isn't straight!" Karl defended himself, motioning for Evan to come take a look.

"Do you see this?" he said, pulling his friend into position next to the wall. "Look at how curved that is."

"Oh, wow, yeah," Evan said, noticing a bow in the drywall. "That's crazy."

"Right? Now imagine trying to make straight pieces of flooring work against that."

"Again, why you didn't phone—"

Karl laughed. "It won't happen again."

"It looks great."

"Nicole loves it," Karl nodded. "So," he lowered his voice. "How are you and Amy doing?"

"Good," Evan said, looking at his girlfriend across the room.

"She's still teaching?"

"Yep, she loves it."

"Are you..."

"Am I what?"

"Are you—" Karl searched for the words. "You know, serious? Do you think you guys are going to get married?"

Evan laughed. "I have no clue! I barely got a solid job; I'm not really thinking about that yet."

"But you've been together for over a year."

Evan shook his head. "I know you want me to be just as happy as you are with Nicole, and I promise. I'm working on it."

"Work faster," Karl said, punching his shoulder.

Just then, the doorbell rang, and Karl took the few steps across the entryway to open it. Aarov and Leena walked in, and greetings echoed around the room. Nicole's eyes widened, and she rushed toward Leena.

"Is this—?" she gasped, holding up Leena's left hand. "You're engaged!?"

Leena laughed, and Aarov puffed out his chest.

"Okay, Karl, take their coats; I need to hear everything!" Nicole said excitedly, throwing Leena's coat toward him.

Karl turned toward Evan, his outstretched arms ready to be piled high with outerwear.

"Could've been you, buddy," he grinned.

Evan laughed, resisting the urge to stick out his foot as Karl passed him and walked into the den.


THE NEXT TWENTY MINUTES PASSED QUICKLY, FILLED MOSTLY with delicious food and more details than Evan ever could've hoped for about Aarov and Leena's engagement. Turns out, Aarov was more of a romantic than he'd given him credit for. He watched Amy's face as Aarov described how he'd arranged for an after-hours ride to the top of the Calgary Tower.

Crap. Now I have to top that somehow? "Hey," he said,

taking a sip of his water, "I thought Alexis was bringing drinks? Where is she?"

Nicole shrugged. "Last I heard, they were on their way—"

As if on cue, the front door opened and Alexis, Tate, and Victoria walked through the front door. The girls carried two paper bags each, while Tate juggled a bag of ice.

Karl jumped up from his seat. "Let's put that on the back porch," he said, taking the bag from him. "It's too bad we don't have a big freezer..."

"Hey, working on it, remember?" Nicole called after him. "What is all this?" she asked, intrigued as she stood and walked toward Victoria.

"Do you happen to have a spot for a French soda bar?" Alexis asked, shimmying with her paper bags.

Nicole laughed, peeking inside one of them. "I put a table for drinks right there, so have at it."

Evan stood, willing to help with anything to get away from the current conversation. "Want me to open up these bottles?" he asked, picking up the one labeled 'French Vanilla' as soon as Alexis pulled it from the sack."

"Sure," Alexis said absently, hurriedly unloading.

As Evan unscrewed the top and pulled off the first seal, the doorbell rang again. Karl—having just walked back into the room carrying a bowl of ice—reached for the handle. Evan turned his head slightly as the door opened and froze.

Was that *Amanda*? The last time he'd seen her had been...was it back in February? And she didn't look like *that*. He observed her as she walked into the entryway. Her dirty-blond hair was pulled up into a loose bun, and her skin looked perfect. Did she still have the scar above her left eye? He couldn't tell from here. She was wearing a v-neck tan sweater and dark bootcut jeans, with delicate silver hoop earrings.

"You've only done one?" Alexis said next to him, pulling the bottle from his hands.

"Oh, sorry," he said, blinking and turning back to the table. He quickly picked up another bottle and resumed his task.

"Amanda," Nicole said behind him, "I'm so glad you made it!"

Alexis put down the bottle she was holding and spun around, leaving Evan to keep working—slowly—on the drinks.

"Almost didn't," Amanda said.

"Did you have something else going on beforehand?" Leena asked.

"No," Amanda answered, not giving any further clarification. It wasn't needed, as far as Evan was concerned. He knew exactly what she meant.

"Well, grab a plate," Nicole instructed, walking her through all the items on the buffet table, specifically highlighting Amy's fudge. "You've met everyone here, right?"

"Get over here!" Alexis said behind him, and Evan lifted his head as Amanda approached the table. Her eyes locked on his over Alexis' shoulder and his heart started beating faster.

Last time they'd met, she'd been in a wheelchair. And the time before that...Memories of that night regularly flashed into his mind, usually in the middle of the night. The feeling of her hand in his—completely vulnerable—as he openly let his guard down and told her ridiculous stories. Right now, the way she looked at him...he wondered if somehow she remembered it, too.

"It's so good to see you. I miss our adventures," Alexis said.

"I know. Though, I'm sure you still have them."

Alexis grinned. "Do you want a French soda? I think we're ready."

"Sure, thanks."

"What flavor do you want? Nicole, you want one too?"

Nicole nodded, "Raspberry, please."

Amanda looked toward the bottles. "Surprise me," she said.

Alexis nudged Evan with her elbow. "You heard the girl," she said, handing him a cup already filled with ice and soda.

Evan glanced at Amanda, then back to the flavors. Surprise her. He turned to ask her a question, but Amy stepped between them.

"I haven't met you either," she said. "I'm Amy, Evan's girlfriend."

Evan's cheeks flushed as he reached for the blackberry syrup.

"Oh, hi," Amanda said sweetly.

"It's so good to put a face to a name," Amy said, then turned toward Evan. "Will you make me one, too?" she asked.

"Sure," he said, clearing his throat and watching as Alexis added milk into the cup he was holding. "Here you go." He handed the red plastic cup to Amanda, and she took a sip.

"Mmmm. What is this?"

"Blackberry and Vanilla."

She smiled, then turned with Nicole back to the group and found a seat next to Leena.

"Sounds lovely," Amy said next to him. "I'll do the same."

He nodded, taking another cup from Alexis's outstretched hand.

At eleven-thirty, after playing the series of horrifyingly embarrassing games Nicole had cooked up, they filled up their plates with seconds on the food and played musical chairs with the available seats in the room. Amanda landed the spot next to Leena again and gratefully took a bite of butter tart. It had been surprisingly easy to forget about last year with this group. Especially since they were all so willing to make a fool of themselves.

She glanced at Evan and then hastily looked away. He was cute. Really cute. And also dating the same girl from last year, per Nicole. That meant it was serious.

Half of this group had visited her at home a couple of months after the accident. That was during what she liked to call her 'bitter phase.' Her hip hadn't healed from the accident, and using a wheelchair was quite possibly her very own hell on earth. She had no idea how she'd acted that day and wondered if she'd made a horrible first impression. She must not have been too bad if Nicole was willing to hang out with her again, but Nicole was kinder than most.

"It's almost officially a new year," Karl announced. "I want to hear what we have to celebrate."

"Then you have to go first," Nicole said excitedly. "Have you told everyone?"

Amanda looked at him with interest. Nicole had mentioned he'd been applying to dental school again but hadn't heard any other updates.

Karl grinned. "I got in at U of A."

Everyone cheered and shouted congratulations, but Aarov held up a hand. "Wait, so that means—"

"They're moving," Evan said. "I know. It sucks."

The energy in the room dulled considerably.

Karl sighed. "Okay, Edmonton is only three hours away—"

"But it's Edmonton," Alexis groaned.

"C'mon, you guys. How often do we see each other anyway these days?" Karl said. "We can still talk and text, and we'll totally have our party again. Not here, obviously, but Aarov and Leena are going to have a new house by then, and he assured me they'd be glad to host."

Leena laughed, and Aarov shook his head. "What about Evan?" he laughed. "He already has a house!"

"A bachelor pad. With zero furniture," Evan laughed.

Amanda grinned, watching the way Evan's eyes crinkled when he smiled. That voice. She felt tingles each time she heard it.

"We'll figure it out, I promise," Karl said. "Aarov and Leena have something to celebrate if you didn't hear earlier."

Leena held up her hand, and everyone cheered again.

"Not only that, this woman just landed second chair violin with the Philharmonic," Aarov gushed. "Even better, I'm still working for TransCanada, so we're *not* moving," he added with a dramatic flourish of his arm.

Amanda laughed and cheered along with the others. She didn't have the history they did but—for tonight—it felt good to be included.

"Hey," Victoria said next to her. "Nicole told me your lease might be coming up at the end of January?"

"Yeah," Amanda nodded, leaning closer. "They're raising the price. It's ridiculous."

"Well...what would you think about moving in with Alexis and me?"

Amanda's eyes widened. "You guys have an extra room?"

"When Nicole moved out, we didn't want to deal with finding another roommate, but it's a three-bedroom. Rent was cheap, and it was nice not having to share a bathroom. So, that's the one negative. You'd have to share a bathroom with me or Alexis."

"Why are you wanting another roommate now?"

"It would be nice to have cheaper rent. I'm fairly positive that split between the three of us it'd be cheaper than what you're currently paying. Our landlord is old and not up on rent prices in Calgary," she laughed. "That would make it incredibly inexpensive for us, and—" she shrugged. "Alexis says you're cool."

Amanda grinned. "I'm flattered. Let's definitely talk about it."

"Here, what's your number," Victoria asked. "I'll phone you, and then you'll have my number. You have Alexis' right?"

Amanda nodded and gave it to her, partially tuning in to the conversation around her. Maybe it was time for a change. She loved her roommates, but they didn't have a lot in common.

After exchanging information, Amanda listened to the laughter around her and filled up a plate with more food. She didn't have much to contribute, and that was okay. It was entertaining to watch Victoria laughing with her friends, Alexis and Tate surreptitiously groping each other, Aarov and Leena reveling in the newness of their engagement, Karl and Nicole playing the gracious hosts, and Evan...well, that was the exception. Somehow, more fudge ended up in her mouth each time she saw Amy resting her hand on his arm or whispering something in his ear.

As midnight drew near, she chose a popper from the

basket Nicole passed around. Was it a new year already? Karl started the countdown at twenty seconds to midnight, and tears unexpectedly sprang to her eyes. She wished Mike could've been here. Because this was exponentially better than last year.

## 3

# DECEMBER 31, 2001

"You don't have to plan this party exactly like Nicole," Aarov teased, snapping a towel at Leena as she rushed past.

"But she always has such good food!" Leena complained. "You think people are going to want to eat pupusas all night?"

"We have more than pupusas. And pupusas are delicious."

Leena rolled her eyes. "Nicole is bringing the butter tarts, but I think we need one more dessert."

"How about cookies?"

"What kind?"

"Good ones."

"Helpful, very helpful, Aarov," she said, pulling a tablecloth over the table she'd set up next to the piano.

"Ooh! Popcorn!"

She stood up. "Caramel?"

"Or peppermint white chocolate, remember we had that at the booth at the Stampede?"

Leena grinned. "Perfect! Yes, I'll look up the recipe and go to the store. Can you pop me a bunch of popcorn?"

"Of course, because I'm *very helpful*," he said pointedly.

She ignored him. "I'll get out a few big bowls." Rushing past him, she stood on tip-toes to pull an old ice cream bucket and two metal bowls from the shelf. When she turned, Aarov was standing behind her. She smiled and kissed him on the cheek.

"You're the best husband. I'm sorry I'm a little—" she shook her head back and forth.

"This party is going to be great, with or without food, so take a deep breath," he said softly.

"Ooh! Candles. We need candles!" she said, pulling away from him and running down the hall.

*"That's her," Aarov said, pointing toward the stage.*

*"The one with long black hair?" Karl asked.*

*"You can just say the Indian one," Aarov teased.*

*"She plays violin?" Mike asked.*

*Aarov laughed. "Let's hope so."*

*"So you've never talked to her before?" Karl asked, aghast. "And you're going to marry her?"*

*"It's not like it's a fully arranged marriage," Aarov said. "Just that my parents and her parents think we should at least consider it."*

*"And you're willing to do that?" Karl asked.*

*"You've met my parents," Aarov said with a sigh.*

*"I think it's beautiful," Mike said. "I wish my parents would choose a girl for me."*

*Karl shoved his younger brother playfully. "Yeah, okay. Mom would choose some girl who loves to make wreaths and knit."*

*Mike laughed. "I don't know; I think there's something cool about trusting people enough to listen to their opinion about who you're dating."*

*"Well, from now on, I'm going to give you all of my opinions on who you're dating. One-hundred-percent honesty," Aarov said, putting a hand over his heart. "That girl you brought to the lake a few weeks ago? Drop her. She was way too high maintenance."*

*"She kind of was," Mike grinned. "I like this new system. Karl, can we comment on Nicole?"*

*"Shut your mouth," Karl said, laughing and pulling him into a headlock.*

*"Boys, this is a respectable venue," Aarov said with mock formality. "Please exude some element of decorum, or I'll need to sit between you."*

*"Ooh!" Mike called, straightening his hair. "She's picking up her instrument. I'm guessing by the end of this concert, you're not going to care who set you up."*

*Aarov watched Leena flick her hair behind her back and settle her violin between her chin and her shoulder. Her skin seemed to have a golden glow in the lights, and her dark brown eyes were intense as she fixed her gaze on the conductor. Mike was right. He was already sunk.*

"WHY IS IT SO COLD HERE!" ALEXIS GROANED, PULLING ON A fleece over her sweatshirt.

"Stop whining," Victoria said, rinsing her cereal bowl and putting it in the drying rack on the counter. "If you hate it here so much, why don't you just move to Haiti."

"Don't tempt me," Alexis warned. "You guys, I can't overemphasize how life-changing this trip was."

"Really?" Amanda laughed, "Because I feel like you've

been doing a lot of emphasizing. Also, we've been paying your rent, so..."

Alexis laughed. "I know, you two are amazing. Thank you for funding my life-changing humanitarian trip."

"You still haven't shown us those photos you were talking about," Victoria said.

Alexis's eyes lit up. "Sit down! I'll get my computer. I downloaded them from my camera last night."

Amanda picked up her piece of toast and sat down on the couch, leaving a space between her and Victoria.

Alexis hurried into the room with her laptop in hand, settling in between them, looking like a puffy, multicolored marshmallow with all her layers.

"Okay," she said, pulling up her files. "This is where I lived."

Victoria's jaw dropped. "You lived there? It's a shack!"

"That's *nice* compared to where the locals lived. I had a roof that didn't leak!"

"What was it like on the inside?" Amanda asked.

"I'll show you," she said, scrolling past a few landscape photos. "Here."

The image came into focus and showed rows of beds with mattresses that looked anything but comfortable.

"You all slept in there?" Victoria asked.

"Yep. The bathroom was outside, and so was our cooking area."

"Did you have to cook?"

"No, a few of the women from the village cooked for us while we worked. I think it was their way of saying thank you."

"And you got an entire hospital up and working?" Amanda asked in awe.

"I mean, 'hospital' is a strong word, but compared to

what they had? Yes. It may as well have been Foothills. We're hoping to fund an x-ray machine there by the spring—"

"Wait," Victoria said. "Are you planning on going back?"

Alexis took a deep breath. "I'm dying to. But the only position they have next year would require me to be there for five months."

Amanda whistled. "Five months? Wow. That's a big commitment."

Alexis nodded. "Is Ben coming here tonight?" she asked, changing the subject.

"Yeah, he said he'd be here around four-thirty," Amanda said. "You two want to drive with us?"

"Definitely," Alexis said, closing her computer. "I need to grill this guy. How did you meet him again?"

"He was in my Cognitive Psych. class."

"He's a nice guy," Victoria said. "You're lucky you met him before you graduated."

"You're telling me. It only took a year-and-a-half to get back on the dating wagon," Amanda teased.

"Worth the wait," Victoria said, waggling her eyebrows.

"Wait, is he hot?" Alexis said, her head snapping back and forth between the two of them.

"I mean—" Amanda started, grinning.

"He IS!" Alexis cut her off. "I need to see a picture ASAP."

"I can pull up his Myspace page," Amanda said, standing and walking over to the desk in the kitchen.

"No, on second thought—" Alexis said dramatically, "I want to be surprised. Don't show me."

"You sure?" Amanda teased.

"Positive."

"It's not fair at all," Victoria complained. "I didn't meet *one* guy worth dating in my hygienist program."

Alexis laughed out loud. "And you're surprised by that?" Victoria's brow furrowed.

"Seriously, how many guys were in the program to start with?" Alexis continued.

"Like, two," Amanda laughed from the kitchen.

"There were more than that," Victoria scoffed.

"C'mon, we all know the real dating pool is going to come when you start meeting dentists," Alexis said, standing and setting her laptop on the table. She walked past Amanda to the sink and filled up a glass with water.

"Yeah, the fifty-year-old *married* man I work for is super dateable," Victoria said.

"Just wait 'til he hires an associate..." Amanda said, and Victoria grinned. "Okay," she continued, "I have to shower and get ready for my ultra-hot boyfriend."

"Ugh, get out of here," Alexis said, and Amanda ran down the hall before her friend could snap her with the dishtowel.


"HE'S SERIOUSLY WAAAY HOT," ALEXIS WHISPERED INTO Amanda's ear as they approached the car. She eyed Ben's broad shoulders, six-foot frame, and shaggy hair peeking out from under his toque.

"Shhh!" Amanda said, slipping into the backseat with him. She slid over to the middle seat and cuddled up to his left side, shivering from the cold.

Alexis shook her head, put the veggie tray and sparkling apple cider on the seat next to her, and then shut the door. "How old are you, Ben?" she asked, sliding into the passenger seat of Victoria's Rav4.

Victoria started the engine and quickly pulled on her driving gloves before reversing onto the street.

"Twenty-three," he said.

"Yes, Alexis, I'm older than him," Amanda muttered, "but only by a year and a half."

"Does that weird you out?" Alexis asked, grinning and turning to face the back seat.

"Not in the least," he answered, kissing Amanda's cheek.

"Cheesy, but I'll let it pass," she teased. "And did you graduate this semester, as well?"

"No, I've still got three semesters left."

Alexis' eyes widened.

"I was on a hockey scholarship and didn't apply myself the first year," he explained. "Then, I had to figure out what I wanted to do."

"And you landed on Psychology?"

"I'm a Sociology major, actually," he said.

"That's great," Victoria cut in before Alexis could begin her rant about the viability of a degree like that. "Have you met anyone besides us who's going to be at the party tonight?"

"I haven't had a chance to introduce him," Amanda said. "Karl and Nicole only came down for Thanksgiving for two days, and they spent it with family."

"We were supposed to go out for dinner with Aarov and —what's his wife's name?" Ben asked.

"Leena. Yeah, that didn't work out because she got sick or something," Amanda said.

"Oh, was that for Aarov's birthday?" Victoria asked.

"Mmhmm," Amanda nodded.

"What about Evan?" Alexis asked. "How's he doing these days?"

Amanda felt her cheeks flush. "The last time I saw him was when we were at the Stampede," Amanda said. "He was with Amy, remember?"

"Oh, that's right. Did they only come that one night?" Alexis said.

Amanda nodded, remembering that entire, whimsical month. First, the trip to Canmore for the wedding. The beautiful outdoor pavilion strung with crepe paper and filled with pastel flowers, Leena's dress—gorgeous. And the party hadn't stopped there. As soon as they got back from their honeymoon, they'd all gone to the Stampede together for almost a week straight. Evan had been there the night they went to the grandstand show. She remembered because she'd sat next to him, and they'd talked the entire evening.

"Didn't Nicole say Evan and Amy broke up?" Victoria asked.

Amanda's heart started beating faster, and she shifted positions to avoid making her agitation obvious. "I didn't hear that," she said. "When did you two talk?"

"Just a couple of weeks ago."

"I guess we'll find out for sure tonight," Alexis said.

Amanda suddenly wished Ben wasn't beside her. Then she felt like a terrible person for thinking that. The light turned green, and Victoria drove through the intersection, pulling onto Sixteenth Avenue heading east.

"I don't even know where Leena lives now," Alexis said.

"That makes two of us," Ben teased. "We should stop at Peter's; I'm dying for a burger," he added, pointing at the sign ahead of them.

Amanda smacked his arm playfully, ignoring his comment. "Did they move after you left?" she asked, and Alexis nodded.

"It's beautiful," Victoria said. "You're going to love it."

.  .  .

FIFTEEN MINUTES LATER, THEY PARKED ON THE STREET IN front of Aarov and Leena's split-level. Amanda and Ben followed Victoria and Alexis up the walkway and front steps, their shoes crunching over the refrozen snow.

"You're not going to leave me alone in there, right?" Ben said, throwing an arm over Amanda's shoulders.

"Pretty sure you can fend for yourself," she teased.

"How's your hip?" he asked, glancing down. "I know it aches when you get cold. And it was freezing in her car."

Amanda smiled. "It's okay, thanks for asking." His sweet comment only made her feel worse for wanting to ditch him in the car.

Leena opened the door, bathing the concrete landing in a warm glow. "Come on in!" she said excitedly, stepping back into the hall. Even from their vantage point on the step, they could see the twinkle lights and garlands strung up in the house. It looked sophisticated and cheery.

Alexis walked in first, wrapping her friend in a warm hug. "I missed you!" she said, stepping back and pulling off her coat and scarf. Her chestnut hair fell in loose curls around her shoulders, and Amanda noticed new, blond highlights from her month and a half in the Caribbean sun.

Leena embraced Victoria next, her arm accidentally hitting Victoria's glasses askew. The women laughed, and as Leena turned, she noticed Ben stripping off his warm outerwear.

"And who's this?" Leena asked, stepping away from Victoria.

"Ben," he said, holding out a hand. "I've heard a lot about you."

"Good things, I hope," she said.

Ben laughed and nodded.

"Are Karl and Nicole here yet?" Amanda asked, setting her boots on the mat.

Leena hugged her and shook her head. "They were out in Airdrie visiting his parents earlier. They said they'd be a little late."

"You guys did an amazing job in here," Alexis said, walking into the spacious living area that flowed into the kitchen.

Leena's eyes lit up. "There used to be a wall here," she said, motioning between the two rooms. She launched into their renovation process, and Amanda followed her across the room. Only partially listening, she caught Evan's eye. He was standing next to the island covered in red and gold Christmas decor and plates of hors d'oeuvres.

"Hey," he grinned, smiling and walking toward her, passing Victoria, who was setting their veggie plate between a shrimp cocktail and a bowl of marinated olives. His eye caught Ben for the first time, and his grin faded slightly.

"Hi, Evan. This is Ben," Amanda said, and Ben moved close to her, wrapping an arm around her waist.

"Hey, man," Ben said.

"I heard you graduated," Evan said.

"I did," Amanda smiled.

"Feels good, eh?"

"Definitely. But I'm going right back in for my Master's."

Evan's eyes widened.

"Not in January, I'm still applying. But I hope to start in September."

"That's awesome," he said, taking a bite of something that looked like spinach dip from his plate. "And then what do you want to do with that?"

Ben patted her shoulder, motioning to the food.

"Go for it," she said. "I'll be there in a sec." Turning back to Evan, she answered, "I'm not entirely sure. I'm debating whether I should do a Ph.D. Alberta is one of the few provinces that doesn't require that to practice, but it still would afford me more opportunities."

"Sheesh. How many years would that take?" Evan asked.

"Like five to eight?"

Evan whistled. "That's a big commitment."

She shrugged. "What about you? You're still working for Solium?"

"Mmhmm, we made our first public offering this year. We'll see how that goes. I've been talking to a guy that went to school with me. He's an electrical engineer, but he has kind of a cool idea for a startup."

"What is it?"

"It's a web discovery platform. I don't know the details exactly, but it sounds like it would basically search the internet for you and provide content recommendations."

Amanda nodded, impressed. "Sounds wild. I can't believe how many internet companies there are these days."

Evan laughed. "I know. And nobody knows what to expect going forward. Especially with all this insanity happening in the world. Kind of risky, but that makes it fun."

"Totally." she grinned. "I'm not sure I'm cut out for that kind of volatility, but I think it's exciting."

Evan reached for a cracker and dip.

"Hey, where's Amy tonight. She was with you when we met at the Stampede, right?"

"She was," he nodded slowly. "Umm, we actually broke up last month."

"Oh, wow, I'm so sorry. What happened?"

"I've just been working a lot, and with her schedule, it was getting hard to find time to see each other."

"She's still teaching, right?"

Evan nodded. "I work late most nights, and she starts early. And really, that's kind of the easiest explanation. There were other issues, too—otherwise, I'm sure we could've made that part work."

Amanda smiled gently. "Are you doing okay?"

"I'm the one who broke it off, but it's still hard to be single again."

"You *are* getting pretty old," Amanda teased, and Evan laughed out loud.

"Thanks for that."

"I'm kidding. You still look like you did when I first met you," she said, her heart unexpectedly dropping as she finished the sentence. The image of her sitting in a wheelchair and meeting Mike's brother and friends flashed through her brain. And how she felt the first time Evan spoke—

"I highly doubt that," Evan grinned, flattered.

Amanda blinked. "I'm going to get some food," she said, a bit off-center. "It's nice to see you."

"Jack Nicholson!" Aarov shouted out, laughing hysterically at Karl's impression of Jack peeking around the door in *The Shining*.

"Time's up!" Leena shrieked, holding out the sand timer triumphantly.

"How many did we get?" Karl asked, still breathless.

"Seven!" Aarov announced.

"I don't know; I think you cheated on Tom Hanks—you totally made a sound," Alexis accused.

"It was an accident!" Karl argued.

"We'll let it pass, but that's your warning," Leena said,

raising an eyebrow. "That makes the score thirty-two to thirty-eight, boys lead."

Before the men's section erupted into cheers, Nicole stood and held up a hand. "We still have one more chance," she said, pointing to Amanda. "All we need is six to tie, seven to win."

"Are you sure you want your hopes to rest on me?" Amanda laughed. "We can choose someone else."

"Nope, it's your turn," Victoria said. "Go for it."

Amanda groaned. "I'll do my best." She stood up and put her hand in the bowl, pulling out a slip of paper. Celine Dion. Easy. When the timer started, she held her hand in front of her face and pretending to sing into it emotionally, then balled her free hand into a fist and dramatically thumped her heart. The girl team yelled out Celine's name, laughing hysterically.

She quickly moved on to the next name, and then the next. When Aarov warned them time was running out, she was moving on to slip number seven. Her heart pounded frantically, and her hands were shaking as she read the name. Oprah Winfrey. How in the world? This name hadn't been pulled since round one.

Thinking quickly, she ran toward Evan, who happened to be the closest person to her. Squatting next to him, she plastered a severe and intent expression on her face and pretended to interview him. When the girls weren't getting it, she pointed to him and threw her hands up in the air, then ran backward and pretended to drive a car toward him, then handed him the keys with an overly excited smile on her face. She then pointed at the next person on the couch and celebrated, then drove their car over and handed the keys.

"OPRAH WINFREY!" Nicole shouted, barely beating Aarov who yelled "TIME!"

Amanda collapsed on the floor, laughing and completely exhausted by her performance.

"SUCKERS!" Alexis goaded as all the women slapped two-handed high-fives.

Amanda sat up and walked back to the couch, joining her team's celebrations.

"That was amazing," Victoria said. "Great job."

"Great guessing, you guys nailed it," Amanda laughed.

"Alright, alright, settle down," Karl roared, feigning annoyance. It's only ten minutes 'till midnight, so grab your snacks or your kissing buddy and get ready to count down.

Victoria rolled her eyes. "I guess that means snacks for me."

Amanda attempted to meet Ben's eyes across the room, but he was engaged in an intense conversation with Aarov.

"Whatever. I'm right there with you," Amanda said. "Did you try those fried, mashed potato things?"

"So good, eh?" Victoria grinned.

They walked into the kitchen and began choosing a few favorites before they completely disappeared from the plates.

"Have you tried these—?" Amanda turned to ask but found herself unexpectedly looking at Evan instead of Victoria. "Oh, sorry. I thought Victoria was right behind me."

Evan smiled. "She got distracted." He motioned to Leena, who was pulling Victoria down the hall. "Probably more renovation talk. I did try those, though, and they were just okay for me."

"Oh," Amanda looked back down at the platter of puff pastry in front of her. "Thanks for the heads up." She reached over and picked up a few cucumbers and olives instead.

"That performance was pretty impressive."

Amanda shook her head. "I don't think I've laughed that hard in a long time."

"Neither have I. I'm not sure if it was because it was such a close game or what, but that was hilarious."

Amanda turned to face him. "I see how it is; you're not willing to give me and my masterful acting skills all the credit?"

Evan chuckled and picked up cheese toast. "I'm just saying. Emotions were heightened."

Amanda's grin faded as she studied him, realizing this may be her only opportunity to talk with him in private. "Can I ask you..." she trailed off, unsure how to phrase her question.

"What is it?" Evan asked, standing straight and holding his plate in front of him.

"I—I wondered if you still have moments where things feel—" she swallowed, her face growing hot.

"Terrible?" he asked, finishing her sentence.

She nodded. "I know it's been two years. And I should be better or something, but I still sometimes feel anxious about driving. And I have these dreams—"

"Don't get me started on the dreams," he said, a sad smile on his lips. "Mine still come at least a few times a month. I'm not sure if the planes crashing into the twin towers made them worse, but I swear since September, they've been even more consistent."

"Me too!" she said, thinking for the first time about the news she'd watched for a week straight. "I hadn't thought about that. What are your dreams like?"

"I—" he stopped short, interrupted by Karl's voice

behind them, giving a two minute warning. Taking a deep breath, he continued, "I don't know if I could describe them." He blushed, seeming to consider his next words.

Before he could continue, motion caught her eye, and Amanda turned to see Ben waving toward her.

"I think you're being summoned," Evan said, laughing lightly.

"Looks like it. Maybe we could talk about this more another time?"

Evan nodded.

"Happy New Year, Evan."

"Happy New Year," he said as she passed. "Hey," he called after her.

Amanda turned, stopping mid-step.

"You're not alone."

She nodded, pausing before continuing in her trajectory toward her boyfriend. Setting her plate on the side table, she began to lower herself to the cushion when Ben reached out and pulled her onto his lap.

"Twenty—Nineteen—" the countdown started across the room.

"Your friends are cool," Ben said, his face inches from hers.

"I'm glad you agree."

"Aarov invited me to play pickup with them next week."

"Hockey?"

Ben nodded, a goofy smile on his face.

"I can tell you're pretty upset about that."

He leaned in and brushed his lips against hers.

"Hey, it's not New Year's yet," she grinned, pushing him away.

"Nine—Eight—"

Ben reached for her, and she fought him off, waiting for

the count to get to 'one.' When it did, she kissed him, losing herself in the moment. Definitely not noticing the eyes that were on her from across the room.

*"So, when you're not feeding baby mountain lions or skipping class, what do you like to do for fun?" Amanda asked, taking a bite of her burger.*

*"Depends. What season is it," Mike asked seriously.*

*"Let's start with summer."*

*"I'm at the lake for a few weeks for sure."*

*"Which one?"*

*"Usually Koocanusa, just over the border."*

*"What do you do there?"*

*"That one, we usually camp and go boating."*

*"For a few weeks?"*

*Mike nodded. "My dad's a high school principal, so he has most of the summer off. We've done it every year since we were kids."*

*"Sounds amazing. So what about when you're not at the lake."*

*Mike chewed his bite and swallowed. "I like to hike. Anything outdoors. I got a new camera last year for Christmas, so I want to take it out and get some good shots."*

*"I know nothing about photography."*

*"I think I can help you with that," Mike grinned, reaching for a french fry.*

## 4

## DECEMBER 31, 2002

"We have to go, Mom," Karl said, pulling on Nicole's arm. "Can we continue this conversation tomorrow?"

Deb put her hands on her hips. "I'm trying to help your wife with her catering business."

"I know, and we both greatly appreciate it, but we're going to be late."

"She had a great idea for transporting those icebox cakes —" Nicole started, but Karl twirled her around in a circle on the way to the stairwell.

"Tell me all about it. Once we're driving."

Nicole laughed, following him to the front door.

"Is this the fourth year in a row you've held this party?" Deb asked in wonder. "Has it been that long..."

Karl walked back up the stairs and put his hands on her shoulders. "Are you going to be okay tonight without us?"

Deb nodded, pulling her sweater closed around her. "I'm going to watch *Law and Order* and then join your dad in bed."

"Do you think he's actually sleeping in there?" Karl asked.

She shrugged. "He's still really sore. I wouldn't be surprised."

"Well, phone if either of you needs anything. We're only going to be in Silver Hills."

"Where's the party at?"

"We booked it at Montana's this year," Nicole answered. "Everyone's busy, and we're trying to make it low stress."

Karl patted his mother's shoulder and returned to the entry, slipping on his shoes.

"Do you think this party is going to keep going?" Deb asked. "With all of you moving on in your lives, I mean?"

Karl stood up and slipped his winter coat on over his sweater. "I hope so. I don't know why, but it helps me stay connected to Mike, you know? Having fun, celebrating together, playing stupid games—" he stopped, dodging Nicole's punch to his shoulder.

"I guess we'll just enjoy it while we can," he said.

Deb smiled. "One year at a time."

Karl smiled and put his arm around Nicole's shoulders and turned toward the door.

"Ooh! Wait just a second!" Deb called behind them.

Karl turned and waited for her to return to the top of the stairwell.

"Here," she said, carrying Mike's camera in her hand.

"Mom, I don't—"

"Karl, Mike wanted to fill this roll of film with happy pictures. We need to fill it."

"But he wanted nature photos, and I'm not really—"

"It doesn't have to happen immediately. Please. Will you help me with this? Just watch for moments that Mike would've loved."

Karl hesitated but then reached out and held on to the camera strap.

"WHAT DO YOU THINK?" NICOLE ASKED AS THEY DROVE DOWN East Lake Boulevard.

"Hmm?" Karl asked.

"About what your mom said. Alexis is already gone this year. Do you think everyone else will slowly fizzle out?"

Karl shook his head. "I don't think anyone will do it purposefully. They all love it. But I know we may end up all over the place. Evan's start-up is going nuts right now—"

"I know. How many times did he go to San Francisco since the summer?"

"Four. Who knows if he's eventually going to move there."

"Aarov and Leena are here to stay, I think."

"Well, especially since she bought into that studio. Seems like a long-term commitment."

"Victoria's coming tonight, right?" Karl asked.

"Definitely. However, she's not thrilled about showing up single again. Last year, she and Evan were the only people without a significant other."

"Evan's definitely not single this year."

Nicole rolled her eyes. "Is he still dating—what's her name?"

"Erin," Karl laughed.

"What is with that? I know she's attractive, but seriously?"

"They work together."

"Not an excuse."

Karl signaled and waited for the traffic to clear before

turning on to Deerfoot Trail toward Calgary. "Don't be too hard on her tonight."

"I'm kind of glad Alexis isn't going to be there. I doubt she'd be able to withhold her comments."

"Well, at least Amanda isn't bringing anyone either."

"I'm telling her you said that," Nicole laughed. "I'm excited to find out how her master's is going. We were supposed to talk last month and then you had that dinner. We never put it back on the calendar." She paused, watching the headlights ahead of them. "I hope she's not going to have an issue with Erin."

"Why would she?"

"I don't know. I've kind of always felt like there was something between her and Evan."

Karl gave her a quizzical look. "What are you talking about?"

"You've never noticed that? There's like an—energy around them. Like they slow down when the other person is close. Does that make any sense?"

"No. None whatsoever," Karl laughed.

"Maybe I'm crazy, then," Nicole said, and Karl reached over, taking her hand in his.

"Not crazy," he said. "You just read too many romance novels."

"I do not!" she laughed, squeezing his hand. "But now I'm going to be watching them extra closely tonight. Just to prove you wrong."

"Prove away," Karl said. "That would be awesome if they got together."

"I knew you didn't like Erin," Nicole muttered.

Karl grinned. "Tonight's going to be amazing. I can already feel it."

❄

"KARL, STOP! THAT HURTS!" MIKE YELLED, HITTING HIM IN THE *chest as he darted to the other side of the room.*

"Well, stop trying to read this!" Karl shouted, his face flushed. "I'm sick of you always getting in my business!"

Mike stood against the wall, breathing hard. "Your business is cooler than my business," he spat, adjusting his shirt.

"I don't care! You need to give me my space."

Mike stuck out his tongue and stomped to his bedroom, slamming the door.

WITHIN MINUTES OF KARL FINALLY SITTING DOWN TO FINISH *reading the note Melanie had passed him in class, Mike was back. This time standing in front of him with his head lowered.*

"I'm sorry, Karl," he said softly, twisting and untwisting his fingers. "I'm nine. And you're thirteen. I know I'm not cool like your other friends, but you are so cool, Karl. You're my best friend. I hate it when we fight, and...I was hoping...can we still be friends if I promise not to read your notes?"

Karl stared at his little brother. "Mike," he said slowly, "you don't need to be sorry. I'm sorry. Of course we're still friends." He patted the cushion next to him. "Promise you won't say anything about this?"

Mike nodded hopefully, his blue eyes still misty with tears.

"Check this out," he said, pulling the note open. "Can you smell that? I think that's her perfume."

"Did she draw those?" Mike asked, pointing at the hearts around the edge of the paper.

Karl nodded.

"She probably loves you," Mike laughed, pulling his knees to his chest. "I hope a girl loves me someday."

❄

Amanda walked into the restaurant and glanced around, looking for their group. Country music blared overhead, and she smiled at the wagon wheels and old-timey pictures on the walls.

"Can I help you?" the hostess asked cheerily.

"Yeah, I'm looking for a group—should be under Karl? Or Nicole?"

The hostess nodded, her blond curls bouncing above her shoulders. "Walk straight down this aisle. They're at the back."

"Thank you," Amanda said, following her instructions. As she neared the back of the restaurant, she spotted them. Evan and a woman she didn't recognize were seated around a large table. Great. This wouldn't be awkward at all.

"Amanda!" Evan greeted her, a little too over-the-top. He stood and hugged her. "This is my girlfriend, Erin."

"Hi," Amanda waved, sitting in the seat across from them. "How long have you two—"

"Almost six months," Erin said, her red lips arching into a satisfied smile. "This guy rocks my world."

Amanda forced a smile to her face, taking in the woman's platinum hair, unnaturally tanned skin, and fake eyelashes. "That's great," she said, turning to hang her coat on her chair. "How'd you meet?"

"Work," Erin laughed. "He noticed me right away."

I'm sure he did, Amanda thought. "What do you do there? I know Evan is in charge of investor accounts—unless that changed?"

"Nope, although I've taken on a few other roles here and there," he said.

"I'm an administrative assistant to the CFO," Erin said

proudly, lifting the menu in front of her. "Have you been here before?" she asked Evan. "What should I get?"

Amanda pretended to look down at her menu, but she couldn't focus on the words. Her mind flashed back to the previous spring when she'd met Evan at Prince's Island Park for the day. They hadn't done much—just walked around and enjoyed the beautiful twenty-degree weather in the middle of March—but after she'd broken up with Ben, she wanted to take him up on his offer to continue their conversation from the party...

*"Do you remember that night at all?" Evan asked, shoving his hands in his pocket as they walked along the river.*

*"What night?"*

*"The night of your accident."*

*Amanda cringed just thinking about it. "The only things I remember are anxiety-inducing."*

*"Like?"*

*"Horrifying sounds, sirens, flashing lights, beeping machinery, scared faces whizzing past ceiling tiles..."*

*"Not the best."*

*They walked in silence a moment until Amanda hadn't been able to help herself. "I remember your voice."*

She could see it perfectly in her mind. Evan had stopped and turned toward her but didn't say anything. Her heart was beating so fast it hurt.

*"I don't remember anything specifically," she explained, swallowing hard, "but when you visited—when I was still in the*

*wheelchair—the first time you spoke. It was like I knew you. Your voice was...comforting, I guess."*

*"I stayed with you that entire night. Your parents didn't get there until the next morning."*

*Amanda nodded, remembering her mom's face the next day when she woke. They'd been visiting family in Saskatoon for the holidays and had come as soon as they could.*

*"Why did you stay?" she asked.*

*Evan thought for a moment. "Deb was anxious about you, and when I saw you lying there all alone...I don't know. It was weird, right? But I guess it felt like the right thing to do."*

THEY'D TALKED THE REST OF THE AFTERNOON, NEVER REALLY delving into anything deeper after that, just laughing about work and life. Sharing their best 'getting back to sleep after nightmares' tips. She'd fully expected him to phone her after that day. He never did.

"WHAT DO YOU THINK?" ERIN ASKED, HER ABRASIVE VOICE breaking into Amanda's thoughts.

"Hmm?" she asked, looking up.

"I wondered if you had any thoughts on the pulled pork sandwich?" Erin repeated.

"I'm sure it's good," Amanda said absently, retreating again behind her menu. *Where was everybody else?*

As if on cue, Victoria's voice sounded behind her.

"Happy New Year's everyone!" she said, sitting down next to Amanda.

Amanda breathed a sigh of relief. "How are you? I haven't seen you in *so* long!" she teased, reaching over to hug her friend.

"I know, those ten hours were killer."

"What were you up to?" Evan asked.

"I'm starting at a new practice near Okotoks, so I was helping set up for the grand opening."

"A hygienist who helps the owners set up? That's got to build job security," he commented.

"That's the goal," she said, blushing slightly.

Amanda raised an eyebrow. She'd suspected something else was at play with Victoria and this new practice, but with that reaction, she was sure of it.

"Hey," Erin said, giving a small wave.

"Erin, right?" Victoria said. "Nicole told me you'd be here tonight."

Erin looked pleased as she hung on Evan's left arm.

"Looks like we're just waiting on the old, married couples?" Victoria said.

"Looks like it," Evan said. "Amanda, what are you up to these days?"

The question grated. It hadn't been *that* long since they'd met up, and it's not like her life had drastically changed since then.

"I'm still working on my Masters," she said. "Slow and steady."

"We made it!" a voice called from behind, and Amanda turned. Leena was walking toward them in a white, wool coat and matching beret, closely followed by Aarov in a black puffer coat and plaid scarf. Nicole and Karl were only a few steps behind him.

"Everyone's here," Amanda said, standing to greet her friends. Excited chatter filled their table as the newcomers settled in and found their seats.

"I'm kind of glad we're a smaller group tonight," Nicole said, scooting closer to the table. "And this is awesome that they sat us at a round table. We can all talk to each other tonight."

"Do you think they're going to let us stay for four and a half hours?" Aarov asked skeptically.

"As long as we keep ordering food," Karl laughed. "It's kind of nice to be at this point, isn't it? Where we're not super poor anymore—oh wait, we're the only ones who are still poor."

The table erupted in laughter.

"Evan's paying for us tonight, right man? You've got plenty to spare."

Evan grinned. "You know I'd always—"

"No way," Karl said, cutting him off. "I'm kidding. Dental school is all debt anyway, so what's another hundred dollars?"

Nicole laughed. "He talks big, but he's gotten SO stingy! I'm making money now, and he still doesn't even want to buy good toilet paper."

"How's your business going, Nic?" Leena asked.

"Surprisingly well, but I'm still figuring out how to organize it. I think I came up with too many menu options, and I need to pare it back down. Make it more streamlined."

"Are you mostly catering for families or private events?" Victoria asked.

"Both, but I'd say events make up more of my business right now. And I think I want to keep it that way. It's more convenient to do volume instead of having to put together smaller orders for multiple families."

"We had an event at our office catered a few weeks ago; we should've hired you instead," Erin said, smiling broadly.

"They live in Edmonton," Evan whispered.

"I know, we could ship it, right?"

"Not ideal in the food business, but that's nice of you to

think of us." Karl said charitably. "Nicole's killing it," Karl continued, putting an arm around his wife's shoulders. "With basically zero help from me."

"Would you like to order drinks?" a male server interrupted, standing next to the table with a pen and pad of paper.

"I'd like a Margherita—double shot please—and—" Erin said, and Evan leaned over to explain as she continued to order.

Karl waved him off. "You're driving, right?" he mouthed to his friend, and Evan nodded.

Everyone else ordered waters, strawberry lemonade, or pop, and Erin looked around quizzically but didn't say anything.

When the waiter left, Aarov spoke. "It isn't fair that we don't get a rematch on last year's games."

Amanda grinned. "We need to meet at restaurants from now on so our win will live in infamy."

"No way," Karl said. "We'll get it back. I'm sure next year will be less crazy, and one of us can host."

Leena and Aarov looked at each other. "I don't know if we'll be an option anymore," Leena said. "It looks like my parents will be moving in this year."

"Oh, wow," Victoria said. "When did that happen?"

"We've always known it would probably happen at some point, but didn't think it would be this soon," Aarov said. "They're having trouble taking care of themselves. It makes more sense this way."

"Are they going to live in the basement?" Evan asked.

Leena nodded. "We just need to fix it up a bit down there—put in a kitchenette. We didn't renovate that when we moved in, and I think it will be best for them to have their own space."

"Isn't there a separate entrance to the basement?" Victoria asked. "I thought I saw that last time we were there."

"Yep," Aarov said. "It will be great. We won't be completely in each other's business."

Drinks arrived, and the server began taking their appetizer orders. Since they weren't in a hurry, Amanda felt no rush to decide on an entree yet. The group ordered two different kinds of poutine, potato skins, pulled pork nachos, and spinach dip. Despite having to stare at Erin's cleavage all night, Amanda was beginning to think this could be an enjoyable evening.

"So who was this Mike guy? That's why you have this party, right?" Erin asked, and Amanda immediately began to feel sick.

"Mike is my brother," Karl said. "He died on New Year's Eve in 1999."

"So sad," Erin said, taking a sip of Margherita from her straw. "How did he die?"

"He was hit by a drunk driver," Nicole said, and immediately realization dawned on Erin's face.

She shrugged. "Wasn't someone in the car with him? Evs, didn't you say—"

"I was in the accident with him," Amanda said, irrational anger beginning to bubble up within her. Why was Evan with this girl? She was vapid and insensitive. Was he attracted to this?

"Ooh," Erin said, leaning forward, "I want to hear all the details."

"You know, I'm actually not feeling that well right now," Amanda said. "I think I'm going to head out."

She stood and gathered her coat as tears began to sting her eyes.

"Amanda—" Leena said, but Amanda shook her head.

"I love you guys, Happy New Year." She walked briskly toward the front of the restaurant and out the front door. She felt slightly bad about leaving the others with her appetizer order, but it wasn't enough to propel her back in there. Even as she walked to her car, she knew she was overreacting. It wouldn't have been a big deal to say 'I don't want to talk about it,' but the whole situation felt overwhelming. Watching Evan with her, listening to her stupid comments —she balled her hands into fists and held back a frustrated scream.

"Amanda?"

She whipped around in the parking lot.

"Evan, just go back inside," she said tersely, searching for her keys in her purse.

"No," he said, walking closer. "I'm sorry about what she said—"

"It's not really about that," she said, starting to shake with the overload of emotions flowing through her.

"What is it about then?" he asked. He wasn't wearing a coat, and she paused, taking him in. He didn't look like the Evan she remembered. He looked like someone out of a Banana Republic magazine, especially next to Erin. If this is who he was becoming at his new job, she wanted nothing to do with it.

Her fingers finally found her key ring, and she pulled it out. "Nothing. It's freezing out here. Go enjoy the party."

"So you're just going to leave? Spend New Year's by yourself."

"Pretty much," she said under her breath, unlocking her door.

"That's such a cop-out. I can fill Erin in, and we don't have to talk about it. Think of Mike—"

"Think of Mike?" Amanda whirled on him. "How about you think of Mike next time you bring someone like *that* to our party." She turned angrily and sat in the driver's seat, slamming her car door. Starting her car, she peeled out of the lot before she could see his face.

## 5

# DECEMBER 31, 2003

"We are officially done for the year," Jesse said, throwing his gloves in the trash. "Thanks for your help today."

"No problem," Victoria said, setting the tools they'd used for their half-day of patients in a disinfecting bath. "I didn't have anything going on until tonight anyway."

"Well, Cara owes you big time."

Victoria waved him off, spraying the dental chair and wiping it down.

"What are your big plans for tonight?" he asked, glancing down the hall to the front desk area.

Pausing, Victoria looked up. "I'm going to this annual New Year's party with friends."

Jesse nodded nervously and took a deep breath. "Listen, I don't normally do this—in fact, I've made it a general rule that I don't ever date members of my staff, but I'd like to take you out sometime if you're interested."

Victoria adjusted her glasses, the wind knocked out of her. She'd worked exclusively with Dr. Storm since taking this job, and she loved every second of it. There'd been many a day where she'd sat grinning in the lunchroom after a morning of playful banter or working extra hard to focus after getting a subtle breath of his cologne.

Though she'd wished something more could happen between them for months, she'd convinced herself he wasn't interested. In her weakest moments, she'd even concocted pretenses in her mind that would allow them to spend time together alone, but always chickened out. That was quite possibly a fast-track to getting fired, and she loved this job. Needed it.

She knew the risks of dating in the workplace, but right now, in this moment, she couldn't have cared less. Jesse was smart, funny, a fantastic dentist, and most importantly, a really decent human being.

"Do you have plans tonight?" she asked tentatively, snapping herself back into the cleaning routine.

"Not anything solid," he said.

"Would you want to come to this party with me? And before you answer," she said, holding up her hands, "know that these are friends I've had for *a long time*. They're not always on their best behavior, and this party started because my friend's husband's brother was killed by a drunk driver on his way to the celebration. It might be kind of awkward." Victoria fiddled with the spray bottle in her hand.

Jesse laughed. "That's quite the recommendation."

She shrugged sheepishly. "Just wanted you to know what you're getting into...if you say yes."

"I'm pretty sure I know what I'm getting into," he said softly, and Victoria's face flushed. "I'd love to come. Can I pick you up?"

She nodded, her voice stuck in her throat.

"You'll need to send me your address," he said, raising an eyebrow.

Her heart was hammering so hard in her chest she could barely breathe. "I can text it to you," she squeaked out. "Party starts at six o'clock."

Jesse knocked his hand on the doorframe, smiled, and walked down the hall to his office.

Victoria stood in stunned silence a moment—attempting to catch her breath—before hurriedly organizing the remainder of the exam room. After saying a quick goodbye to Jesse and the office staff, she ran to her car and immediately dialed Nicole's number.

*"Okay, you didn't tell me Karl was bringing a group of friends over," Victoria huffed. "Nicole, I have finals I'm studying for!"*

*"They're not staying long, I promise. And it's only Evan and Karl's brother, Mike."*

*Victoria looked out the window to confirm. "How long is 'not long,'" she asked, eyeing her roommate skeptically.*

*Nicole laughed, "We're just going to decide on what to do; it was annoying trying to talk to everyone over the phone, so— since I'm driving anyway—I told them to come over, and we'd figure it out here."*

*"Is Alexis going?"*

*Nicole nodded.*

*"So you're saying I'll have the apartment to myself?"*

*Again, Nicole nodded. "Just twenty minutes or so, then you won't have to deal with us."*

*"Fine," Victoria sighed, just as Karl knocked on the door. She sat in her chair and opened her laptop, pulling out her notes and refusing to make eye contact so as not to attract attention.*

*They walked inside, and Karl and Evan followed Nicole into* the kitchen. Karl's brother, however, walked toward her and sat down in the chair next to her. She kept her eyes trained on the screen, but discomfort bubbled in her chest.

"Hi," she said finally, at least acknowledging him.

He waved. "I'm Mike, Karl's brother."

"Victoria," she said. "Why aren't you in there?" she asked, nodding toward the kitchen.

"I'm kind of just tagging along; they won't take my opinion into account anyway," he said, and she looked up. "It's not a big deal. I really don't mind. I think it's cool that Karl lets me hang out with him all the time. And I love doing everything he loves, so...it works out."

Victoria nodded. "Well, I'm studying, so I'm sorry I can't chat."

"What are you studying?"

"Anatomy."

"Human or a different species?"

She looked at him quizzically. "Human."

"Sweet, that's the easy stuff. Want me to quiz you?"

She stared at him. "How old are you?"

"Twenty."

"Are you a biology major?"

"Undecided."

"Sure," she said hesitantly, handing him her computer. "I'm working on the nervous system."

Mike grinned. "Do you love 'On Old Olympus' Towering Top, A Finely Vested German Viewed a Hawk?'"

Victoria blinked.

"You've never heard that before? It's a mnemonic for the cranial nerves. Here, I'll write it out," he offered, reaching for the pad of paper and pencil on the coffee table.

Victoria watched him in awe. Who was this kid? And why wasn't he coming over more often?

❄

"THIS ONE-HUNDRED-PERCENT LOOKS LIKE A BACHELOR PAD, no offense," Nicole laughed, stepping inside Evan's house.

"None taken," he grinned. "If it didn't, wouldn't you be a little concerned?"

Karl set down the bags he'd been carrying and pulled his friend into a hug. "Long time no talk, man! What've you been up to the past few months?" He took off his shoes and hauled the bags into the kitchen.

"Just work, work, and more work."

"And clearly hitting the gym," Karl teased.

"A little bit of that, I guess."

"You look great, Evan," Nicole said.

"Don't get any ideas, babe," Karl laughed, pulling an impressively large bag of Doritos to the counter while Nicole arranged the butter tarts on a disposable platter.

"Any ladies in the picture these days?" Nicole asked seductively.

"Nope, definitely not," Evan chuckled. "I don't have time to date right now. And honestly, I haven't met anyone worth finding the time for."

"Is Erin still working at your office?" she asked.

Evan nodded.

"Awkward?"

"It was for the first few weeks, but then she got over it."

"She's a little crazy, eh?" Karl said, balling up the grocery bags and shoving them under the sink.

"That's an understatement."

"I don't get it," Nicole said, putting the lid back on her Tupperware container. "Why were you even with her? You're an amazing guy, Evan, and I'm completely blown away you haven't found someone decent yet."

Evan shrugged. "She was fun and—"

"Hot," Karl cut in.

Nicole rolled her eyes.

"That," Evan said, pointing to Karl. "See. He gets it."

"Hot girls are never worth the drama," Nicole said under her breath.

"I thought you were hot!" Karl insisted, pulling her toward him.

"Not *Erin* hot. I didn't have my boobs hanging out all the time, and you hardly ever saw me with makeup on."

"True," Karl laughed. "Still totally hot."

Evan laughed. "I'm sure as soon as I'm not traveling as much, I'll be able to put some effort into potential relationships."

Nicole broke away from Karl's grasp. "You better hurry it up. Otherwise, you're going to be one of those guys. Forty, loaded, hitting on girls half your age—"

"What's so wrong with that?" Evan laughed.

"Okay," Nicole said, feigning annoyance. "You two want to gang up on me? Fine. I'm going to the grocery store. You can have your shallow man conversation while I'm gone."

"Why do you need to go to the store?" Evan asked, still grinning.

"I forgot the cheese plate in Airdrie."

Evan smiled sweetly. "I love cheese. Thanks for doing that."

"Bye, babe! Love you!"

"Uh-huh," she muttered, walking out the door.

When the door closed, Karl turned on his friend. "Okay," he said. "Spill. I know there's something else you're not saying."

"What are you talking about?" Evan said innocently.

"Is it a girl?"

Evan shook his head.

"You've been traveling to San Francisco a lot this year again. Did you meet someone there?"

"No, I promise. I've gone out with a few random girls, but nothing worth writing home about."

"Then what are you hiding? I know I haven't been the best about keeping in touch, but I hope you know—"

"I'm moving."

"Already? Haven't you only been in this house since March?"

Evan nodded, running a hand through his hair. "Garrett is moving the company to San Francisco. We've got a lot of potential investors there. I'm going with him."

Karl's eyes widened. "San Francisco? That's quite the change."

"I know. I'm kind of broken up about it. I know it's right for the company, and I'd be lying if I said I wasn't excited about the financial possibilities for me, but—I don't think I'm ready to leave Calgary, you know?"

"When do you go?"

"February 15th."

"I graduate in a year and a half. Until then, I doubt we'll have the time or money to come visit you—"

"Don't even worry," Evan said, leaning on the granite countertop. "We'll still see each other. I'm already thinking about camping again this summer. We have to keep that going."

"I might have an internship during the summer."

"Even if you do. I'm sure we can squirrel away a weekend or something."

Karl nodded, folding his arms across his chest.

"Where do you think you want to practice once you

graduate?" Evan asked, walking around the counter and sitting on a stool.

"No clue. There's no way we're staying in Edmonton."

"Airdrie?"

"Maybe, we've considered it. Airdrie is starting to boom, so there may be a good opportunity there. And I feel a certain amount of responsibility to stay close to my parents."

"How are Deb and Ray?"

"They're good, plugging along. I think my dad's ready to retire and snowbird it."

"Tell him he can come stay with me in the Bay Area anytime."

"Not warm enough. He needs Arizona or Mexico or something."

Evan laughed. "San Diego's not far."

"True," Karl said, his smile fading.

"You okay?"

"Yeah, I've just been thinking a lot since last year's party—"

"You mean the New Year's scandal of 2002?"

"That one," Karl laughed. "My mom said something before we left about this party not lasting forever, and I completely disregarded it, but...do you think we're going to be able to keep it up?"

Evan exhaled, thinking. "I guess it's realistic to assume that people are going to go different directions, and it might be difficult. But on the other hand, how lucky are we to have a tradition that pulls us all together once a year? It's not *that* big of a commitment. It will depend on if people continue to value these relationships. I know I do."

Karl nodded. "I think it allows me to feel less guilt about moving on with my life. Somehow knowing that once a year,

I'm going to set aside time to remember Mike and do something to connect...I don't know. It helps."

"Then who cares if everyone else continues to show up? As long as you want this, let's keep it up."

*"MIKE, YOU COMING?" EVAN ASKED, LEANING HIS HEAD BACK inside.*

*"No, I've got a thing today," he called from the back of the house.*

*Evan hesitated, then closed the door and walked to the car.*

*"Mike has a thing?" Evan asked, looking at Karl.*

*"Yeah, some African festival at Prince's Island Park. I guess he's going with a group from one of his sociology classes."*

*"He's studying sociology now?" Evan asked, buckling his seatbelt.*

*Karl shrugged. "I can't keep up with what he's studying," he said, putting the car in reverse and backing onto the street."*

*"When was the last time we went to a game without him?" Evan asked.*

*Karl thought for a moment. "Huh," he said. "Probably never."*

*"Kind of weird, right?"*

*"Yeah, that is kind of weird. Whose fries am I going to steal?"*

*"Not mine," Evan laughed, then looked out the window. He didn't know what else to say. Mike usually had some random topic he brought up, and he wasn't in the habit of driving the conversation.*

*"Who do you think's going to win tonight?" Evan asked. At least it was something.*

AMANDA HESITATED IN HER CAR WITH THE ENGINE IDLING. She'd had to drive by herself since Victoria was riding with her new date and Alexis was going out for dinner with friends from work before the party. She'd come a little late, hoping someone else would be here before her. It's never fun to show up to a party alone, but even worse when you're walking into someone's home and you haven't spoken to them in a year. And that last meeting wasn't necessarily pleasant.

Mustering her courage, she turned the car off and took the keys from the ignition, reveling in the heated seat for a few more seconds. Then, swinging the door open, she dropped her feet to the street.

This was a nice neighborhood. She knew Evan was doing well for himself, but buying a house like this seemed a little surreal. Would she be making money someday and not have student loan payments?

Walking up onto the porch, she rang the doorbell. Thankfully, Nicole's was the face that appeared through the storm door.

"You made it!" Nicole greeted her, welcoming her inside.

Amanda glanced around. The house was sleek and modern. Minimalist.

"How are you? I've missed you," Amanda said, hugging her friend after she took off her boots and coat.

"We're great! Well, I'm great. I think Karl's a little burnt out, to be honest. Can you believe it's already been two months since I was down here?"

"No," Amanda shook her head. "We need to plan another girls' weekend. Especially since Alexis is planning to be here this year."

"I know, she's doing such amazing work. What is the non-profit called again? Haiti Arise?"

"Yep. They've already started construction in Haiti for a school."

"That's amazing. And so incredible that she found her calling," Nicole said, walking into the kitchen.

Amanda followed her and immediately noticed Evan standing next to Karl and Aarov. She looked around the room, fully expecting to find a woman she didn't recognize. When she only found Leena, she breathed a sigh of relief. It was still going to be awkward around Evan, but at least she wouldn't have to worry about making small-talk with a stranger.

"Hey, Leena," she said, then looked down and gasped. "Are you pregnant? Is that rude to ask?"

Leena laughed. "I'm six months along, so I'd hope it would be obvious."

"Did you know about this?" she looked at Nicole. "Why didn't you tell me?"

"Leena gave me strict instructions to wait," Nicole laughed.

"I wanted to see your faces when you found out!" Leena said.

"When are you due?" Amanda asked, in awe of her perfectly round belly.

"March thirteenth. But who knows. My mother delivered almost a month early on each of her babies. We've already got the nursery ready just in case."

Amanda heard her phone buzz in her purse. She pulled it out, and her face lit up. "Victoria and the dentist are here. Hey!" she called to the three men. "Be nice to him, okay?"

"Who?" Aarov asked.

"Victoria's date. She's majorly into him."

Evan caught her eye briefly, but she hastily looked back to Nicole and Leena.

"Have you met the guy?" Nicole asked.

Amanda nodded. "I saw him for about five minutes when I went in to get my teeth cleaned. He's cute."

The doorbell rang, and the three women rushed to the door together.

Victoria stepped inside, followed by a tall, handsome man with dark hair.

"Ladies, this is Jesse. My dentist—" she stopped short, blushing. "I mean, the dentist I work with at the office."

"I came in a few months ago," Amanda said, reaching out and shaking his hand.

"I remember you, Victoria's roommate, right?" Jesse smiled. His teeth were immaculate.

"I was Victoria's roommate before I got married. You'll meet my husband in a second," Nicole explained.

"And I'm just a friend," Leena said, extending her hand.

"Oh my gosh, Leena—you're pregnant!" Victoria exclaimed. "How did—I mean, I know how—" she said, somehow blushing even more deeply than she had before, "but when? How far along are you?"

Nicole motioned for Jesse to set their coats on the chair, then walked with him and Amanda into the dining room and kitchen.

"Let me introduce you to everyone," Nicole said, approaching the men next to the counter. "Aarov, Evan, and Karl—that's my husband—this is Jesse, the dentist Victoria works with."

"Nice to meet you," Karl said, shaking his hand.

"I hope you know we're not going easy on you just because you're new," Aarov said. "You're going to have to play the games and everything else—"

"I've heard the stories," Jesse cut in, amused. "Victoria already warned me."

Aarov looked at Victoria, appalled. "You gave him a heads up? That's no fun!"

Victoria shrugged, walking toward them. "You guys better be nice."

"We're always nice," Evan teased.

"Did you meet my wife?" Aarov asked as Leena stopped next to him.

"I did," Jesse nodded. "I think I've met everyone at this point."

"Not me," a voice said behind them, and Karl led the group in over the top cheers as they turned to greet Alexis.

"You're here!" Nicole said, rushing to her.

"Wow, I'm coming late every year," Alexis laughed. "Best 'hello' ever."

"We missed you!" Aarov shouted dramatically across the counter. "Last year wasn't the same."

Amanda cringed thinking about last year's drama and her early exit. It wasn't the same for so many reasons.

*"ARE YOU KIDDING? APOLOGIES ARE ABSOLUTELY THE MOST important part of any relationship,"* Mike asserted.

*Amanda walked next to him on the trail, her eyes dazzled by the brilliant red, orange, and gold leaves all around her.*

*"But don't you think that's a weird way to answer that question?" Amanda laughed.*

*"Nope," Mike said.*

*"I thought you'd say 'selflessness' or 'compassion.'"*

*"But apologies cover all of that," he said, stopping to take a drink from his water bottle. "You can't truly apologize if you're thinking of yourself. And you have to have compassion for someone if you're willing to do it. Apologies cover everything—*

*good communication, commitment, honesty—it's all there. If you can't apologize to someone and if they can't apologize to you? Red flag right there."*

"Hey, Evan?" Amanda said, walking across the room. "Can I talk to you for a second?"

Evan nodded, stepping away from Aarov and Karl.

"How are you?" she asked, delaying the awkward acknowledgment of her behavior she knew was coming.

"Good, you?"

His smile was disarming, and she cleared her throat. "I just wanted to apologize. For last year. I know we haven't talked, but—I don't know what got into me. I was emotional about a lot of things, and I didn't handle it well. I know that's not an excuse. I was rude. To both you and your date. And I'm sorry."

Evan's face was unreadable. "Thank you," he said. "I'm sorry, too."

She nodded, turning on her heel.

"You were right, though."

She looked at him quizzically.

"Erin wasn't a good fit for me or our party."

Amanda tried to look repentant. "Should I say sorry for that too?"

"We're good," he said, obviously amused.

Amanda walked back over to help Nicole set up the food, breathing a massive sigh of relief.


Amanda stifled a laugh watching Victoria and Jesse as the clock struck midnight. They clinked their glasses together and then fell into a clumsy dance, trying to decide whether to hug, shake hands, or nothing at all. She had to turn around entirely to avoid spitting out her water when she saw Karl taking a picture of it.

Alexis moved around Aarov and Leena to sit next to her, and she couldn't have been more grateful.

"Happy New Year, friend," she said, taking a bite out of a butter tart.

"Happy New Year. What are your predictions for 2004?"

"Hmmm...I predict...that we're all going to learn more about ourselves, be slightly better humans than we were this year, and that we'll all do some good in the world."

Amanda smiled at her. "I think those are predictions I can get on board with." She saw Leena yawning as Aarov picked up their plates and took them to the stainless steel garbage can in the kitchen.

"You turning into a pumpkin, Leena?" Alexis asked.

"I seriously can't stay awake. This," she said, pointing to her belly, "sucks the life out of me."

"You made it to midnight, right?" Amanda said, giving her a thumbs up.

"Success," she said with drooping eyelids.

Aarov returned and put his hands on her shoulders. "Let's get out of here."

"Happy New Year's, everyone!" Leena said, standing and waving, resting a hand on her belly.

"We have to get going, too," Karl said, standing and clapping a hand on Evan's shoulder. "We have to be back up in E-town by tomorrow afternoon."

"You have class on New Year's Day?" Alexis asked, horrified.

"No, I have to catch up on my work before class starts again," Karl said.

Evan stood and pushed his chair back against the wall. "Ah, I see how it is. You've been slacking."

"That's the way I would describe Karl. Such a slacker," Aarov said from the entryway, helping Leena zip up her boots.

"Can I help you clean up?" Nicole asked, looking at the kitchen.

"No, you go," Evan said, waving her off.

"I can help," Amanda offered. "Apparently, I'm the only one cool enough to have zero plans tomorrow."

"I can help, too," Alexis said, clearing the bowls of snacks from the coffee table.

"Is it alright if we take off?" Victoria asked hesitantly. "Both of us worked today, and—"

"Get out of here," Alexis said. "Jesse, you're cool. Loved your impression of Burt Reynolds."

"I'm really fine," Evan insisted. "You don't have to stay and clean."

Alexis rolled her eyes and opened his pantry to find the broom.

"Do you have Ziplocs or containers for me to put this extra food in?" Amanda asked, pushing the bowls of extras next to the sink.

"Sure," Evan said, opening a drawer and pulling out options.

Amanda emptied the various bowls and platters, then filled up one side of the sink with warm, soapy water.

"I do have a dishwasher," Evan teased.

"This'll be fast." She scrubbed the dishes, enjoying the Christmas music drifting in from the other room. After spending hours amid loud laughter and boisterous conversation, the peace and quiet felt like an unexpected gift.

"See you at home," Alexis called from the entry, and

Amanda turned her head. Was she leaving already? Glancing around, it looked like everything else was mostly done.

"Okay, I'll be right behind you."

Two more bowls to go. She picked up the first one and started to scrub something sticky off the bottom.

"Did Alexis take off?" Evan asked, walking back into the kitchen.

Amanda felt her heart rate quicken. How had she ended up here alone? She nodded.

"It looks great in here. I appreciate the help."

He walked around the counter and reached next to her to pick up the dishcloth sitting next to the sink. His body was inches from hers and her senses heightened. She scrubbed faster.

Holding the cloth under the faucet, Evan turned on the water and soaked it, then wrung it out and began wiping the countertop.

"What do you have planned for tomorrow? Any exciting New Year's Day plans?" she asked.

"Nope. Just enjoying a day at home. I have to fly out to San Francisco again on the fourth, so I'm going to do as little as possible until then."

"I don't blame you. How often do you have to go?"

"Usually only once or twice a month, but we're gearing up for some big changes, so it's been more frequent lately."

"At least it's an amazing city. Not, like, Saskatchewan or something."

"Hey, don't knock Saskatchewan," he laughed.

Amanda smiled. "I remember when you told me about this startup," she said, rinsing the second bowl and setting it upside down in the sink to dry. "It seems like it's come a long way."

"It has. I don't think any of us believed it would take off like it did."

"That's a good thing, right?" she asked, drying her hands on the towel draped over the oven door handle.

"Definitely. Also, a little crazy."

"I can imagine."

"Hey," he said, setting the cloth next to the sink and looking directly at her. "How are you doing? I haven't heard much about your program or life in general for a long time."

"Probably because there aren't any newsworthy changes," she said, leaning against the counter. "I'm still basically doing the same thing I was two years ago. School, research, teaching a little—"

"At U of C?"

She nodded. "Helping one of my old professors."

"When do you finish?"

"I finished my Masters last month."

Evan's eyes widened. "Wait, you're done?"

"Yep. For now. I'd still like to get my Ph.D., but I think I need to work for a bit first. Get some experience, log some supervised hours, and begin paying off the massive amount of student debt I've collected."

"Is it bad?"

Amanda sighed. "No, not compared to other people I know. I'd saved up quite a bit and had scholarships for undergrad. But it still feels like a lot when I've been making next to nothing for years now."

"I get it," he said, sitting down on a stool.

"No, you don't," Amanda teased. "You've been making good money—clearly—for years."

"It's true," he laughed. "But I was a student once. It was stressful to feel like everything I spent was money I was going to have to pay back at a premium later."

"So you kind of get it."

"Right," he grinned.

Amanda stared at him a moment. His green eyes fixed on hers. What was it about him? Was it some intangible, subconscious physical attraction that made her always a little unbalanced in his presence? Whatever it was, it was getting annoying. Couldn't she just put whatever this feeling was aside and be herself? Just be friends?

"How are your dreams these days?" he asked gently.

"Hmm?" she said, snapping back to the present.

"When we went to the park that day. I guess it was over a year ago, so maybe you don't recall. You were having trouble with nightmares."

Amanda nodded. "Still there, but better. I guess it's true that time heals all wounds. Maybe in another couple of years, I won't get tense when a car cuts me off," she said derisively. "What about you?"

"Here, I want to show you something," he said, motioning for her to walk with him into the living room. He pulled a laptop from the bookshelf and sat next to her, booting it up. "Karl put this together for his parents this year. I think he's planning to send a copy to everyone, but he has to get it burned onto discs first. So, shhh. Don't tell him I showed it to you early, okay?"

Amanda mimed a zipper across her lips. She watched with interest as the video loaded, then inhaled sharply when the title appeared on the computer screen.

*Mike McKay, 1975-1999*

EVAN PUT AN ARM OVER HER SHOULDER, AND HER BODY hummed. Pictures and videos of Mike as a toddler flashed across the screen, and tears began to pool in her eyes. Her emotions jumped to the surface so readily that she immediately diagnosed herself with trauma repression. Not that that was an actual diagnosis, but still.

She watched as Mike got older—watched him celebrating after a win in a hockey tournament and blowing out candles on his birthday. Tears streamed down her cheeks as she saw him in University, exactly how she remembered him. She caught her breath when a picture of her showed up on the screen; that was the first weekend they'd started dating. Where did Karl get this picture?

The montage ended with pictures of the McKay family, and Amanda—out of habit—hastily attempted to wipe the moisture from her cheeks.

Evan turned to her, his eyes red and watery. "Do you know why I wanted to show you that?"

Amanda laughed as new tears began to form. "No! I'm a complete disaster now, so thanks for that."

He put out a hand, stopping her from frantically dabbing her eyes. "It's okay, Amanda. It's okay to feel sad and frustrated and to react poorly sometimes. You apologized earlier for your reaction last year, and I'm grateful. But I wonder if you ever give yourself a break."

Amanda stared at him, the tears continuing to flow down her cheeks. "I took a break after the accident, but it didn't help. I was just miserable, and then behind in school, and—"

"That's not the kind of break I'm talking about. I mean a break from holding everything inside. Have you ever talked with Karl and Nicole about all this? Like about Mike or about what he meant to you?"

"No," she shook her head. "I didn't want to be insensitive. There's a diagram I like that shows the circle of grief, and I'm way on the outside—" she motioned with her hands, but again he gently lowered them.

"I get that you know way more about this stuff than I do. But just as a passive observer? I don't see you letting your guard down. It doesn't seem like you want to be vulnerable."

*"WHAT ARE YOU AFRAID OF?" MIKE ASKED SINCERELY.*

*"What do you mean?" Amanda asked, confusion written all over her face.*

*"Don't get me wrong; this paper's good. But it isn't you."*

*"How do you know that?" she said, raising an eyebrow.*

*"Because you don't talk like this," Mike laughed.*

*"Well, of course I don't. This is a paper—"*

*"No, I get that you need to sound professional, but you're playing it safe. Writing what every other student in there is going to come up with. Though, I'm sure you wrote it better," he winked.*

*Amanda rolled her eyes.*

*"I'm serious," Mike grinned. "It's well-written, but what would you write if you were willing to open up and lay it all out there?"*

*Amanda bit her lip.*

*"Write that," Mike said. "If we're unwilling to feel exposed, then what's the point of literature analysis anyway?*

AMANDA'S BROW FURROWED AND SHE PULLED HER HANDS AWAY from Evan's.

"I can be vulnerable," she said. "I'm a therapist, for crying out loud. I'm simply careful with who I open up to."

He raised an eyebrow. "Who?"

"I meant whom."

"No," Evan laughed, "I'm not correcting your grammar. Who do you open up to? Alexis?"

"She's been gone on and off for the last few years—"

"Victoria?"

"She's always working, and I've been swamped finishing my classes—"

"Then, *who*? I know it's not me, even though—"

"Even though *what*?" she said tersely, anger bubbling up within her. "I'm the one who put forth any effort to get together, and even then, you never phoned me back! You *said* you wanted to hang out again—you brought it up multiple times. And next I see you, you're in a fancy new job with a new girlfriend, and new clothes—"

"You noticed my clothes?"

"Of course I noticed your clothes," Amanda said, her face flushing. "You never used to wear dress pants."

Standing, she marched into the kitchen for a drink of water. She opened three cupboards before finding the right one, then pulled out a glass and filled it up.

"I phoned you," Evan said from behind her.

She took a drink and whirled around. "No, you didn't."

"I did. I phoned the next day. I left a message with Victoria, and she said she'd let you know."

"I didn't get a message. And why didn't you phone my cell?"

"I dropped my cell and had to get a new one, remember? We talked about it that day at the park. Karl only had your apartment number."

Her face went blank. He did mention it was broken.

"Why didn't you try reaching out again?" she asked, not nearly as self-righteous as she'd been moments before.

"I didn't want to seem completely desperate!" he said, running a hand through his hair in frustration. "And that's not the point. The point is, you asserted I didn't phone, I'm saying I did." He looked at her, exasperated. "Why didn't you get in touch?"

Amanda took a deep breath. There was a dull throb behind her eyes, and she glanced at the clock. One in the morning. No wonder she was so emotional.

"This is not the time for a conversation like this, Evan. I'm tired and—"

"No," he said, standing and walking toward her. "Why didn't you?"

"Evan, I—" she started but closed her mouth. What was she supposed to say to that? "Okay, you want vulnerable? Here it is. I'm attracted to you, okay? I felt uncomfortable phoning because I knew what I was feeling and—because you didn't contact me—I then knew with absolute certainty you didn't feel the same way." She stopped to catch her breath. "I didn't want to make a fool of myself. Like I am right now."

Evan walked closer, his eyes fixed on her. "But I did phone," he said, his voice low.

"Well, yeah, I know that now, but—" her voice caught in her throat as he stepped closer and slipped an arm around her waist. Her pulse quickened as she stared up at him, his face barely an inch from hers.

With one swift motion, he closed the gap between them and tentatively brushed his lips against hers. Her head was spinning, and she fought to keep herself upright. Trailing her fingers up his arms, she kissed him back, feeling the curve of his shoulders as she looped her hands behind his neck.

He felt just as she'd imagined he would, and her mind

raced. How often had she fantasized about kissing him? If she'd known back then he had any feelings for her, she would've phoned him in a second.

*Did he have actual feelings for her now?* Or was he just desperate on New Year's? No, this was precisely the kind of thinking she'd fallen prey to last time. Those rationalizations led to her shoving everything down and convincing herself she didn't care what Evan did or didn't do.

But oh, she definitely cared. She cared that his lips were pressing hungrily against hers and that his shirt smelled faintly of vanilla. She cared that she could feel his chest rising and falling quickly next to her as he pressed her against the countertop. She cared that his hands were pressed against her, slightly lifting the bottom edge of her sweater and barely grazing the skin of her lower back.

She cared. And she wanted to care like this more often.

## 6

## DECEMBER 31, 2004

"I'm moving to San Francisco," Evan said, his voice husky.

Amanda's eyes flew open. "When?" she asked breathlessly.

"February."

"So...we can do this until then?"

Evan nodded and lifted her onto the counter—

AMANDA'S EYES FLEW OPEN, AND SHE GASPED FOR BREATH. She lay in her bed a moment, gaining her bearings. She was home. In her own house. Alone.

She hadn't thought about Evan in weeks, but it made sense her brain would replay that torturous memory today of all days. She groaned, rolling over in her bed. How had another year gone by already?

She'd kissed Evan almost every day until he left, and they'd said all the things, like 'we'll talk every day' and 'we can make long-distance work,' but the reality was: he was living in San Francisco long-term. And she wasn't.

After a month or two of being distracted by wanting to

be closer and yet recognizing the impossibility of it, their communication slowly petered out. Evan became more entrenched in his job and busy life in the city while she was increasing her patient base and gearing up to start a Ph.D. It seemed impractical to keep things up.

Her heart still raced when she thought of him, and she was both relieved and disappointed when he'd texted earlier in the week saying he wouldn't be at this year's party. She knew she wouldn't be able to act naturally around him yet. And it wasn't a self-compassionate practice to make out with someone once a year with no strings attached. At least that's what she told her clients.

She didn't feel unsettled when she thought about him anymore, since the initial mystery of what it would be like to be close to him was blown wide open. The downside was that she now knew with absolute certainty what it felt like to be kissed by him...

She flicked off her sheets and forced herself out of bed. Time for a hot shower. And possibly some leftover Christmas cookies.

"JESSE, NICE TO SEE YOU AGAIN," NICOLE SAID, WALKING through the door of Victoria's new apartment.

Victoria took the platter from her friend's hands and walked it into the kitchen.

"Love this place. And the location is fantastic," Nicole said, hanging her coat on the hooks by the front door.

"I know, it makes my commute to work less than fifteen minutes," Victoria said excitedly.

"And the trip to my house only five," Jesse said, grinning.

Victoria blushed. Somehow, after dating for nearly a

year, he could still make her heart race with comments like that. She took his hand, and the group walked into the living room. Karl and Nicole sat on the loveseat next to her grandmother's piano, and she and Jesse took the couch.

"How's the practice going?" Karl asked.

"Great," Jesse answered. "We just added another associate, and I'm down to four days a week."

"Sounds ideal," Karl said. "Victoria, you realize I'm graduating in the spring."

Victoria nodded. "Yeah..."

"And you're a fantastic hygienist."

"I am," she grinned.

"So, you're going to come work for me, right?"

Victoria laughed out loud.

"That wasn't meant to be a joke," Karl said, smiling broadly.

"Karl, you know I'd love to work for you. But I'm taken at the moment."

"Stupid Jesse," Karl muttered good-humoredly.

"Are you planning to open your own practice?" Jesse asked.

"I don't know. Seems smart to work for someone for a bit, get my feet wet."

"That's what I did. I worked for a guy over in Springville for a couple of years. It's nice because you start to understand what you want and what you don't want in every aspect of a practice. Then when you branch out, it makes those decisions easier."

Karl nodded. "Actually, my old dentist in Airdrie is looking for an associate. My mom was in there last month, and he brought it up."

"Is he close to retirement age?" Jesse asked.

"He's past retirement age," Karl laughed. "Still plugging away."

"You might get lucky. You could buy the practice from him and not have to start totally from scratch," Jesse said.

"But then we'd have to live in Airdrie," Nicole teased.

"C'mon, I grew up there. It's not that bad. And it's growing like crazy," Karl argued.

Victoria watched them go back and forth and grinned. There was a comfort there, an ease. Neither of them seemed to be holding back their real feelings or criticizing the other person for theirs. She didn't know if she was there with Jesse yet. Though she couldn't realistically expect to be after only a year. Karl and Nicole had been together for—was it almost six years now?

The doorbell rang, and Victoria stood to answer it. Leena and Aarov stood behind the glass with a fluffy bundle in their arms. She opened the door and ushered them in, peeking under the blankets to catch a glimpse of baby Paul.

"How are you feeling?" she asked Leena.

"I'm great. Paul just started sleeping through the night."

"That's huge," Victoria grinned.

"I know. I feel like an entirely new person."

"New enough to do this again?" Aarov asked, pointing at the baby, and Victoria could tell he was partially—if not mostly—serious.

"Not here," Leena scoffed, waving him off.

"Well, of course not here—"

"No!" she smacked his shoulder. "We're not having that *discussion* here."

Aarov smiled mischievously. "She wants four children; I want eight. Who do you think is going to win?" he asked, leaning close to Victoria as Leena walked toward Karl and Nicole to show off the baby.

"For your sake, I hope it's Leena," Victoria said, and Aarov laughed. Before she could make it to her seat, the doorbell rang again. This time it was Alexis and Amanda. She hugged them and took their food to the kitchen, then polled the room for drink orders.

There were times she missed living with roommates, but as she pulled glasses from her perfectly organized cabinets, her heart leaped in pure delight. It was also incredibly gratifying to organize and find things exactly where you put them.

"Hey, can I help you with those?" Jesse asked, sidling up next to her.

"I'd love some help," she grinned, handing him a couple of glasses from the shelf.

Before she could fill them, shrieks of delight sounded from the other room, and Victoria rushed in to see what was going on. She saw Nicole holding two hands over her belly and an expression of pure elation on Leena's face.

"Someday," Jesse said, wrapping an arm around her waist, "that'll be us."

Victoria's cheeks flushed deeply as she looked at him. He kissed her on the cheek and walked back to the kitchen to assemble the drinks.

"Do you care if I fall asleep on the way home?" Nicole said, leaning the passenger seat back. "The first trimester is no joke."

"Don't you remember Leena last year? Sounds like all of pregnancy is no joke," Karl laughed with loopy energy after counting down the start to another new year.

"Don't you dare say that. I'm hoping it's going to get better in a few weeks."

"Under-promise and over-deliver, right?"

Nicole rolled her eyes. "I missed Evan tonight."

"I know. I get it, though. Flights around the holidays are—"

"He's got the money," Nicole cut in.

"No, it's not about the money. He couldn't find a decent flight that got him in and back fast enough to be back for a couple of important investor meetings. He could've flown out from December twenty-eighth through the thirtieth, but what would be the point of that?"

"At least we could've seen him!" Nicole said indignantly.

"We're going to see him at the end of next month, remember?"

"I know, it's just—it doesn't feel like the holidays without him."

Karl nodded, turning onto Deerfoot Trail heading north.

"I'm a little scared," Nicole breathed.

"About Evan?"

"No—I guess a little—but I was talking about this," she said, pointing to her belly. "What if I'm a terrible mom."

"You won't be a bad mom."

"But I'm already having feelings."

Karl's brow furrowed. "I'm well aware of that—"

"No, like...feelings I'm not proud of."

"What do you mean?"

"I'm worried about my own time. Going to lunch with friends, sleeping in—and I'm nervous about my business. What if I can't keep it up? I've worked so hard to figure all of this out, and I've got a fantastic clientele, and then I'm going to be out of commission for who knows how long, and—"

"Whoa, Nic. I'm so sorry; I had no idea all of this was running through your head."

"Well, it is."

Karl reached out and squeezed her hand. "We felt good about starting a family. And I don't have all the answers to the questions you just posed, but I do know that we're really good at figuring things out."

Nicole nodded but didn't look convinced.

"Remember when Mike died?"

"How could I forget."

"Well, that was crazy, and we both had so many emotions, not to mention the amount of work that needed to be done to help my parents take care of everything. We were both exhausted, maxed out, and it lasted for months. That's kind of how people describe having a newborn, hey?"

Nicole laughed, a sad smile on her lips.

"So, I'm just saying. We went through all of that, and somehow we were still able to work on our rental, get admitted to dental school, pay our bills. We've already proven we work well under stress."

"It's true," she mused. "I guess I'm just scared because I don't know what my body's going to do. What if I don't recover quickly?"

"Then we'll figure it out. It's perfect timing. I'll be finished with school, and we can move back closer to family, and I'll be around to fill in the gaps as needed."

"Thanks, babe."

"You're welcome, babe," Karl grinned, giving his wife's belly a playful pat.

❄

"DO YOU THINK WE'LL EVER BE DADS?" MIKE ASKED, SHOOTING the basketball through the hoop on their driveway.

"Dude," Karl laughed, running to steal the ball from him. "What are you even talking about?"

Mike shrugged. "I don't know. I was just thinking about it."

"Right now? While you're in high school? Shooting hoops on the driveway?"

"Is there a better time to think about it? And you're not in high school anymore. You could be a dad anytime."

"You know how that works, right?" Karl laughed. "It's not happening any time soon."

"But you want kids?" he asked, catching Karl's rebound and dribbling back toward the lawn.

"I think so," Karl said. "Do you?"

"Definitely." He took the shot and missed.

"Do you think about stuff like this a lot?"

"Not a lot, a lot. I'm not a weirdo," Mike scoffed.

"We all know you're not as immature as most kids your age," Karl said, making a jump shot.

"Was that a compliment from my older brother?" Mike asked in awe.

"I said, 'not as.' But yes. You're welcome."

"You miss me, eh?" Mike said, waggling his eyebrows and dribbling around his brother to the hoop.

Karl laughed and walked over to get a drink from his water bottle. "I do, man. I think moving out made me realize how cool our family is."

"By 'family,' you mean me," Mike prodded.

"Don't push it."

Mike grinned and passed him the ball. "P-I-G. You shoot first."

## 7

## DECEMBER 31, 2005

"Those donations should be here Friday," Alexis directed into her cellphone.

"Aren't you worried that we haven't heard anything?" a man on the other end of the phone asked.

"No, I'm really not. I mean, I guess there's a chance they could no-show, but they've been here every year for four years. I highly doubt they're going to ditch."

The man sighed. "I know you're right; I just organized some things at the center the other day, and seeing how empty those shelves were—"

"Hey, I completely get it. But know that I will make sure we get inventory before our new families move in. Come hell or high water, we'll make it happen. Promise."

"Okay, thank you. I'll chill out."

"You do that," Alexis laughed. "And maybe get out and have some fun tonight? People working with refugees tend to burn out quickly, and I want to keep you around."

"I know; me too."

"Alright, then. Have fun; I'll see you on the second."

Alexis hung up the phone and exhaled. No rest for the

weary. She walked into the kitchen to find Amanda wholly engrossed with her cell phone screen.

"What's going on here?" she asked, taking a mug from the hooks underneath the cupboard.

Amanda groaned in frustration. "I can't find anyone to go to the party with me tonight."

"I'm going with you."

"That doesn't count. You're going to be with Brad. That makes me a third-wheel."

"I've been a third-wheel for what, three years running?" Alexis grinned. "It's not that bad." She filled the teapot with water and set it on the stove, then turned on the burner.

"Yeah, well, Evan's going to be there," Amanda said, chewing her lower lip.

Alexis shrugged. "It's been a year and a half. Don't you think—"

"With his new girlfriend."

"Ah. Yeah, okay, I get it."

"Thank you."

Alexis searched through the basket on the counter for apple cinnamon herbal tea. "Who have you asked?"

"Literally everyone I could think of. That isn't a total weirdo."

"And you just started asking today?"

"No, I started asking yesterday. I was talking with Nicole, and she happened to mention that he was bringing a girl from San Francisco."

"Eesh. So she's probably super stylish."

Amanda shot her an annoyed look. "Not helpful."

"Hey," Alexis said excitedly, "what about Taylor?"

"Who's Taylor?"

"You met him. At the Christmas party we worked on together at the shelter."

"Oh, wait, the tall guy?"

"Yep, that's him."

"He's cute."

"That's what I'm sayin'."

"Do you think he'd go with me?"

"I know he's single; want me to check if he has plans?"

"Definitely."

"Should I tell him the whole situation?"

"Most likely. That way, he can *really* play along."

"Wait," Alexis laughed, "you want him to pretend to be your boyfriend?"

Amanda cringed. "Is that weird?"

"Mmhmm. But I bet he would. He's usually up for whatever." Alexis typed the message into her phone. "Sent. I'll let you know what he says."

"Thank you, thank you!" Amanda said, walking toward her bedroom.

"What are you going to do if he says no?" Alexis called after her.

"Probably see if I can get a last-minute boob job," she yelled down the hallway.

"Can't wait to see it!"

Evan sat in the private dining room watching the clock. It was ten minutes past seven, and he was starting to worry that Nicole and Karl had gotten lost. He told them Stephen Avenue, hadn't he? Maybe they were parking. He'd told them just to do valet, but knowing Karl—

"I don't think I've ever seen you nervous," the woman sitting next to him commented. "It's kind of cute."

"Yeah?" he grinned.

"I said 'kind of.'"

"I'm worried some of my friends might find parking down here a little intimidating. They don't come downtown much."

"Do they live in the suburbs?"

"Most of them live in Calgary, but they're a little more—"

"Alberta cowboy?"

"No," Evan laughed. "More down-to-earth."

"They're not Republicans, are they?" she asked with distaste.

"That's...not a thing here. We have a lot of different parties—"

"Still. I'll try to keep the political talk to a minimum."

"Probably a good idea," he said, rechecking his watch, then looking up hopefully as movement near the door caught his attention.

"This place is swanky," Nicole said, walking into the McTavish Room in One18 Empire restaurant.

"I'm glad you like it," Evan grinned, standing from his seat at the long, wooden table in the middle of the cozy room. "I figured it was the least I could do."

"I mean, you could've done a lot less," she laughed, taking in the modern decor and romantic lighting.

"Happy to help. I know Victoria hosted last year, and she's planning a wedding—I wanted to make it easy. Hopefully everyone likes the food."

"It's food; what's not to like?" Karl laughed, clapping his friend on the back.

"Evan," Nicole said softly, placing a hand on his arm. "I'm sorry about your dad. I know you two were close."

"Thanks," he said sincerely, holding her eyes a moment. This is my girlfriend Kayla," he continued, motioning to a woman with long, dark hair in a perfectly-fitted black cock-tail dress.

"Nice to meet you," Nicole said, pulling her into a hug.

Evan stifled a laugh taking in Kayla's face. She'd never been to Canada before, and he probably should've done more to prep her. But this was more fun.

"Is this little Mike?" Evan asked, moving closer to the car seat Karl was carrying. He lifted the cover to find a tiny baby, bundled up and fast asleep. "Hi, little guy," Evan whispered, replacing the blanket. "He's *so* small."

"He's five months old—this is almost triple what he was when he was born."

Evan's eyes widened. "Are you serious?"

"He is on the small side," Nicole added.

"For some reason, I thought you'd met him because of our camping week, but then I remembered he was *born* when we were supposed to be out there," Karl said. "I still feel bad about canceling, by the way."

"Don't. I was so slammed that week; it ended up being a good thing."

"When he wakes up, I'll pull him out so you can officially meet him," Nicole offered. "Maybe we can sit at the end? I'll ask them to bring a high chair so we can set the car seat up off the floor."

As soon as Nicole disappeared around the corner, the rest of the group walked in together, led by the hostess.

"Leena, are you—" Evan started.

"Yes. Twins," she said with fear in her eyes.

Aarov leaned over to Amanda and whispered something in her ear.

Amanda. She looked stunning. Her hair was darker and longer than when Evan had last seen her, and it fell in soft curls around her shoulders. She wore a navy blue dress that flattered her athletic figure, and it took him a moment to tear his eyes away.

"Evan?" Leena said, cocking her head to the side.

"Twins, that's insane," he said, picking up where they left off. "Where's Paul? And how old is he now?"

"He's almost two, and we left him with our parents. Having a baby at a party is one thing, but a toddler?" She raised an eyebrow.

"I'm sure it would be entertaining," Evan laughed.

He hugged Aarov and Alexis, shook hands with Alexis's boyfriend Brad, whom he'd never met, but apparently, they'd been together for a while. Seemed like a decent guy, but was he a few inches shorter than her? Maybe she was wearing heels.

Victoria and Jesse waved as they passed, making their way to Nicole and Karl to see the baby.

Trying not to make it awkward, he moved to greet Amanda and hugged her just like everyone else. But it wasn't just like everyone else. She felt familiar—comfortable—and it took him off-guard. He stepped back more quickly than he usually would.

"Evan, Taylor. Taylor, Evan," Amanda said, motioning between the two of them as she brushed her hair behind her ear.

Evan reached out a hand. He tried not to size him up, but he couldn't help it. Taylor was taller than him. Slightly. He was a little lanky, to be honest, and he looked like a hockey player.

Taylor smiled and put an arm around Amanda's waist. "Shall we find a seat?" he said, and Amanda's eyes sparkled as they passed under the overhead rustic chandelier.

Did he really just say that? Shall we? Who says 'shall

we'? Evan followed them to the table and sat next to Kayla, who'd already found her way back.

"Has everyone met my girlfriend Kayla at this point?" he said to the group, a little too loudly.

Victoria stood at the other end of the table, introducing herself and Jesse.

Amanda gave a small wave as she pulled out a chair across from them. "I'm Amanda; this is Taylor. We must've missed you at the door."

Kayla smiled demurely and folded her napkin in her lap. "Are we ordering apps at some point? I'm starving," she whispered to Evan.

"Already ordered, they were just waiting for everyone to be seated."

As if on cue, the wait staff entered with water glasses and lemons for everyone, then went around the room for specific drink orders. The head waiter caught Evan's eye, and he gave him the go-ahead to begin their meal service.

"Evan, this is *so* nice," Leena said. "Did you tell them to split the checks?"

"No way," he said. "I'm covering this tonight. I haven't seen you all in almost two years."

"But—" Aarov began to protest.

"No way!" Evan insisted. "Just sit back and enjoy the meal. I heard there might be fireworks at midnight, too, so maybe we can do our countdown outside?"

"Sounds perfect," Karl said.

Evan laughed at the irony of Amanda and Taylor sitting directly across from him and Kayla. Not that it was a problem—he'd honestly be glad to hear what she'd been up to the past year—but it still felt a little...raw.

Most relationships he'd been in ended badly, or at least one or both parties was happy for it to end. Not with

Amanda. Had they lived closer, they'd likely still be together. And that made tonight more confusing than he'd anticipated. Apparently, those feelings weren't gone like he'd thought. 'Closure' was something he'd heard others talk about, but it wasn't until this moment that he understood why.

Thankfully, Leena and Aarov were the next ones over— split across the table—and they were feeling chatty, as usual.

"Taylor, tell me about what you do for work," Aarov started.

"I work with Haiti Arise. With Alexis. But now, we're working on growing a few different refugee programs here in the city. I'm the director of that initiative."

"Admirable," Aarov said.

"What about you?" Taylor asked. "I know, Leena, you teach violin at a studio, right? Amanda and Alexis mentioned that."

Leena nodded.

"Of course they'd mention her. Music is much more exciting than what I do," Aarov said, and Leena rolled her eyes. "I'm an engineer. I work in the oil and gas industry."

"You've been hit pretty hard this last year," Taylor commented.

Aarov nodded. "I'm watching it very closely, that's for sure."

Amanda looked concerned. "At this point, could you switch industries?"

"It would be difficult. I've been in this field for so long; it would be hard to convince a company to take me if they had another qualified candidate with more recent experience. But it's not unheard of."

"Well, hopefully, it will be a non-issue," she said sincerely.

"With Martin re-elected, I'm not holding my breath," Aarov quipped.

"You never know," Taylor said. "He might call an early election, and Harper—"

"Wait, say that again?" Kayla said abruptly.

Taylor stared at her.

"He might 'call' an early election?" she asked.

Taylor nodded, perplexed.

"Is that how it works in this country? Leaders can call elections whenever they want?" She looked to Evan for confirmation. This was absolutely more fun.

"There are rules attached, but yes. Acting upon advice from the Prime Minister, the Governor-General can dissolve Parliament and call a snap election."

"Are you sure we can't drink at this party?" Kayla said under her breath.

"You can do whatever you want," Amanda said sweetly, but Evan caught the flash of her eyes as she looked down to pick up her water glass. "Kayla, what do you do? You're from San Francisco, right?"

"I'm not originally *from* San Francisco, but I do live there now. For the past ten years, actually. I'm from upstate New York."

Amanda nodded, looking sincerely interested.

Kayla continued. "I'm the Chief Marketing Officer at our company. Since we've already seen quite a bit of growth over the past few years, I'm mostly focused on retention, engagement, and brand strategies."

"Sounds...important," Amanda shrugged.

"It's one of the most mismanaged roles in start-up

companies, though," she sighed. "And I'd hardly call us a start-up anymore, would you, Evs?"

Amanda's eyes widened, and she cleared her throat, reaching again for her water. He knew she was well aware that he'd hated that nickname. For some reason, when Kayla had initially started calling him that, he let it slide. And now it had gone on too long to fix. It was growing on him.

"You two have one child? Two?" Kayla continued, directing her comment to Aarov and Leena.

"We have one, with two on the way," Leena said, shrugging her shoulders in defeat.

"Do twins run in your family?"

Leena shook her head. "We're the first."

"Do you know whether they're both boys or girls? One of each?"

"We won't know for another couple of months. I feel huge already, but I'm only twelve weeks along."

"Well, there are two growing bodies in there," Amanda said in awe. "I can't believe by this time next year you'll have *three* kids."

"Will you be coming back for Victoria's wedding in the spring?" Aarov asked Evan.

"I don't know," he sighed. "I'd love to, obviously, but I might be in Australia during that time."

"Australia," Amanda asked, "for business?"

"Company retreat," he said. "Technically, there will be some work I'll need to do, but it's mostly for team bonding and morale."

"Our executive team has been working six days a week for a year straight. I'd say we deserve a vacation," Kayla said, and Evan nodded knowingly.

"Alexis," Aarov called across the table. "How can I get involved with donations for your refugee project?"

"You can ask Taylor; he's right there," she laughed.

"You know my parents were refugees, right?" he said, ignoring her comment.

"I do. You'd love what we're doing. You and Leena should come down to the center sometime. Just text me, and we'll set it up."

The whole time Aarov was talking, Evan was sneaking glances at Amanda. Her eyes crinkled in new places, and her jaw was more defined. She fiddled with a small, gold ball on a chain around her neck, and his heart nearly stopped when he recognized it. He'd given her that necklace. The week before he'd left for San Francisco.

AMANDA CUDDLED CLOSE TO TAYLOR OUTSIDE THE MARRIOTT, watching the starry sky for the promised fireworks. Only five minutes to midnight.

"Did I pull it off?" Taylor asked quietly, and Amanda laughed out loud.

"You passed with flying colors, and I owe you big time. Free therapy for life?" she flashed him a cheesy smile.

"I love that you're offering *me* therapy when you just hired a guy to be your boyfriend for the night," he chided.

"Hired is a strong word. I believe you came willingly."

"You're lucky that the meal was delicious."

"I feel fortunate. And grateful. I know this is such a weird situation, but I don't think I could've handled watching those two canoodling all night if I had to do it alone."

"What ever happened with you two? Bad breakup?"

"No," she sighed. "The opposite, actually."

Karl yelled out a two-minute warning, and watching his childlike enthusiasm made Amanda smile. She loved this goofy group of friends, even if it was awkward to see Evan with someone new. And hard to see everyone moving along with their lives when she was still in school and very unmarried and un...pregnant. Victoria and Alexis weren't married yet, but they were closer than she was.

"I had a legitimately pleasant evening," Taylor said. "Thanks for being my pretend girlfriend and inviting me for the fanciest New Year's Eve experience I've ever had."

"Wait, did you hire *me*?" Amanda teased.

Taylor laughed, then looked at her pensively. "Moment of truth. Do I kiss you when the clock hits zero?"

"I'm game if you are," she said playfully.

"I mean, I'm always up for a good snog," he said, grinning.

"FIFTEEN—FOURTEEN—" Karl started up next to them, and as he got to 'four,' the fireworks began overhead. Brilliant, colorful shards split the night sky, and the blasts echoed off the steel and glass buildings.

With lights exploding above them, and cheers in the icy Calgary streets, Taylor held Amanda's face gently between his hands and leaned in.

*"Are you sick of teaching me yet?" Amanda laughed, pulling off her goggles as they walked into the ski lodge.*

*"Never," Mike grinned. "You're doing great."*

*"I highly doubt you wanted to spend your whole day on the bunny hill."*

*They found an empty table, and Amanda stripped off her gloves, toque, and coat. Her feet still felt incredibly unnatural in* her ski boots, but once she sat down, she was able to mostly relax.

"Hot chocolate?" Mike said, holding two steaming styrofoam cups.

"Yes, please."

Mike blew on his drink, taking off his helmet. "You're doing great."

"I might be kind of remembering a few things from when I was a kid...but it's still so scary when I start to go fast."

"It'll come, don't worry. You just need to go a few more times this season so you don't forget everything before next year."

Amanda took a tentative sip of her hot chocolate. "Thanks for this," she said.

"It was a dollar fifty, don't sweat it."

"No, this. This whole day. I've had friends invite me skiing, and I was too nervous to say yes because I knew I'd hold everyone back. Now, at least, I won't stop the chairlift."

Mike smiled at her, his cheeks rosy from the cold. "How much longer do you think you have in you? Lifts close at four."

"I'm going all day, are you kidding? I've got to lower my per-minute cost."

Mike laughed out loud. "Alright, hardcore. I love it."

Their drinks reached a mostly tolerable temperature, and they were able to finish them within a few minutes. After a bathroom break, they dressed and walked back out into the cold.

Amanda walked to the racks to locate her skis. She spotted them and clunked toward them, focusing entirely on remaining upright. Before she pulled them out, Mike appeared next to her.

"Hey," he said, "can you take those off for a sec?" he said, motioning to her goggles.

She pulled them up, confused.

"And pull that down," he said, reaching out and lowering her scarf. He smiled, his blue eyes sparkling in the sunlight.

"What? Did I spill something on myself?" she asked, wiping the sides of her mouth with her glove.

Slowly, he leaned in and slipped a gloved hand behind her neck, pulling her close.

"This has been a wonderful day," he said, his face inches from hers.

Her pulse quickened. "I agree," she breathed.

Mike kissed her then, slowly and meaningfully. Like this joy existed within him, and he was letting her in to share it for a moment. It took her breath away, and for a minute, she forgot she was on the side of a mountain riding pieces of fiberglass across the snow.

## 8

## DECEMBER 31, 2006

"What time does your flight get in again?" Amanda asked, stifling a yawn.

"We're boarding now, so looks like we're on time. Should be at exactly noon," Colin answered.

"Remind me, did you check bags?"

"I didn't."

"K, I'll be there. Want to go for lunch?"

"What time does your party start tonight?" he asked.

"Karl said six o'clock. We should still have plenty of time to get you home in between."

"Sounds good. You pick the place for lunch. I'm just excited to see you."

Amanda smiled, rubbing the sleep out of her eyes. "Me, too. Have a good flight."

She hung up the phone and rolled over, hugging her pillow to her chest. She had legitimately missed Colin over the past two weeks. Not that she didn't think she would, but it was comforting to get confirmation of her feelings.

Closing her eyes, she allowed her mind to run over the highlights of the past year. It'd been a great one. She was building up her practice—even starting to get some word of mouth—and had decided on the topic of her Ph.D. 'Understanding relational stress during periods of grief' wasn't the first title she'd landed on, but found herself drawn to it for obvious reasons. As she'd searched the literature, she'd become hungry to find answers that didn't readily exist, and her dissertation had been born.

She grinned, mentally reliving the moment her body—from head to toe—had prickled with excitement. And that's when she'd phoned Colin.

He was an academic advisor she'd met with when considering another topic. They'd been talking on and off for weeks, and she knew she needed to give him a heads up that she'd chosen a subject outside his field of expertise.

When he answered, she explained the situation and was in the middle of expressing gratitude for his assistance when he stopped her.

*"So you'll be looking for a different academic advisor, then?"* he asked.

*"Yes, I'm so sorry it won't work out, and I appreciate—"*

*"Would you like to have dinner with me Wednesday night?"*

He'd left her speechless. He had to call her name twice before she could make her mouth work again, and when she did, she'd said yes.

"YOU'RE NOT WORKING TODAY, ARE YOU?" NICOLE ASKED OVER the phone.

"No," Alexis answered.

"Is it bad that I don't believe you?"

Alexis grinned. "I might be checking a few emails, but—"

"Ha! I knew it. Put the laptop away right now!"

"What else would I be doing with this time? Sit alone in my empty apartment? Watching some crappy holiday special on CTV?"

"A - they aren't crappy. I'm watching one right now while I bake. B - you wanted to live alone, and C - you could be very not alone if you drove over here and helped me."

"I haven't showered yet today," Alexis laughed.

*"Then you could be doing that with your time."*

"Okay! I'm putting the computer down. I'll shower and drive out there in a bit."

"Want to get the stuff for French sodas? We haven't done that forever."

"Sure, I can pick that up on the way."

"See you soon."

Alexis clicked on one more email, read it, and typed a response. The refugee program had skyrocketed over the past year, but their infrastructure had not. It was still only her, Taylor, and two other admin staff running the show. Sure, they had volunteers at the center, which was incredibly helpful, but it wasn't taking much off her plate.

Setting the computer aside, she added to her mental to-do list. Find a volunteer willing to upgrade their website. Or hire someone. And find someone to be in charge of bookkeeping. Standing up, she walked into her bedroom and dropped her yoga pants in the laundry. She sighed, realizing the bookkeeper had been on the list for a few months already. Maybe she should write stuff like this down or hold a meeting or something. 'Hold a meeting,' she added to her list, then walked into the bathroom and turned on the water.

❄

"MIKE, YOU'LL NEVER GUESS WHAT I SIGNED UP FOR," ALEXIS SAID *excitedly over the phone.*

*"You need to tell me immediately," he laughed. "I'm a terrible guesser."*

*"I'm working with a non-profit! I met this girl who just started this initiative in Haiti. We're going to build a health center in this teeny tiny village—"*

*Mike yelled into the receiver, and Alexis laughed, holding the phone away from her ear. "When do you start?" he asked.*

*"I don't have all the details yet, but I think we're going to spend a significant amount of time upfront getting things going. Then hopefully we'll be able to take a trip down in the next couple of years and get it going!"*

*"That's amazing, Lex. I'm so thrilled for you."*

*"You should come with me," she said. "I know it's a ways out, but you should come."*

*"I wouldn't want to steal the opportunity from someone else, but if you need an extra set of hands, you know I'll be there."*

*"Start saving up," Alexis said, grinning.*

"THERE ARE GOING TO BE SO MANY BABIES THERE TONIGHT," Victoria sighed.

"Isn't that your dream?" Jesse grinned, pulling his wife closer to him on the couch.

"Don't get me wrong, I love holding other people's babies, but I just thought..." she trailed off.

"That we'd be able to make our own announcement?"

She looked at him with sad eyes. "Is that ridiculous?"

"We've only been trying for two months."

"I know, I just thought it would happen immediately. Leena said—"

"Everybody's different. I think it's fairly normal for it to take a few months."

Victoria exhaled, snuggling into his chest. She tried to pay attention to the Law and Order episode on the screen but wasn't successful.

"Do you think I'm too old?"

Jesse laughed. "Aren't you and Leena the same age?"

"Approximately. But she started sooner."

"Are you saying we need to make up for lost time?" he said with a playful grin.

Victoria sat up slightly. "Having sex more frequently doesn't increase your odds of getting pregnant. It's more about timing and—"

"I know," he laughed. "I was kidding."

Victoria took a deep breath.

"I'm taking this just as seriously as you are, I promise. I want to start a family, too. But I don't think we're really in control of this part of it."

"It's true," she said glumly.

"And you can always announce it to your friends later."

"It would've been *so* good to do it tonight, with everyone all together."

"It'll still be good later. Maybe we can throw a Canada day party or something—"

"You think it'll take that long?" Victoria asked in horror.

Jesse laughed out loud, turned off the TV, and pulled her into his arms.

VICTORIA SAT IN HER CAMPING CHAIR ON THE CURB, WAITING FOR *the parade to start. Alexis was sitting next to some guy she met down the street a few days ago, and Nicole was saving a spot for*

*Karl, and possibly Mike. She wasn't sure if he was coming or not.*

*She loved Canada Day, but it was way too early to be up this morning. She'd worked late into the night on applications. She'd taken the prereqs, and now it was time to finally start her program. If she could get in. That was a slightly important detail.*

*"Congratulations!" a voice sounded next to her, and she jumped. It was Mike, standing slightly behind her with a goofy grin on his face.*

*"Hey," Victoria laughed. "What is this?" she asked, taking a small bag from his outstretched hands.*

*"You passed anatomy!" he said with excitement. "So, I got you some Smarties—because you love chocolate and you're smart—a Wunderbar—because you're wonderful and—"*

*"I love chocolate," she laughed.*

*"Right. And a whack-a-Mack because...it's delicious."*

*Victoria was beaming. "Mike, that was seriously so thoughtful," she said, standing to give him a hug. "Thank you for helping me study. Having someone who knew whether I was right or wrong was super helpful."*

*Mike waved her off. "It was a blast. And it saved me from watching those two making out all the time," he said, pointing to Karl and Nicole.*

*"Alright, I guess we're even," Victoria smiled. "Have you decided what you're going to major in? You must have what, almost half of three different majors at least?"*

*Mike shrugged. "We'll see. I'm having too much fun to decide yet."*

*She could hear the marching band in the distance, and it seemed to be getting closer.*

*"Enjoy the parade," she said, waving as she sat back down and opened her Smarties.*

❄

EVAN RANG THE DOORBELL AND TOOK A DEEP BREATH. WHEN the door opened, he bravely walked in and greeted his friends with all the social graces. He followed Karl around as he gave him a tour of the new house and even managed to keep an interested expression on his face. Those ten minutes felt like a thousand.

Most of his left hand had gone numb on the drive over. He knew it would probably fade in the next couple of hours, but that didn't make the experience any less terrifying.

"Kayla couldn't make it this year?" Nicole asked.

"No, she's in Switzerland actually," he said absently.

"Switzerland?"

Evan nodded.

"I didn't realize you were still traveling so much," Karl said.

"I'm not right now, especially since we're looking to sell the company in the spring. This is something she's doing on her own. A sister's trip."

"Since when are you selling the company? To whom?" Karl asked as Nicole walked to answer another doorbell ring.

"eBay. As long as everything goes through."

"Seriously? That's got to be a big payout."

"Fingers crossed."

Evan looked toward the door to see Victoria and her husband walk in.

"People are finally getting here?" Alexis said, untying the apron around her waist and wiping flour off her cheek. "What?" she asked, noticing Evan's smile.

"Nothing, I've just never seen you all—domestic like this."

"A lot has changed over the last couple of years," she said audaciously, walking past him to the entryway.

"Hey," Karl said, his voice low, "are you okay?"

"What do you mean?" Evan said automatically.

"I don't know; you seem...tired. Is that all it is? Are you tired from the trip?"

"My energy's definitely a little low tonight. Sorry. I'll try to pep up."

"No, it's fine. I just wanted to make sure. I know since little Mike came along, I haven't been that great of a friend—"

"You've been a good friend, Karl. Give yourself a break. You've got a new baby; you graduated, moved, and started a new job in half a year."

"It sounds pretty hardcore when you say it like that."

Evan clapped him on the back.

"Karl, can you help me with this?" Nicole called, pointing to the closet door.

"Be back in a sec," he said, and Evan breathed a sigh of relief.

There wasn't much he hated more than small-talk, and now here he was talking surface-level with his best friend. He'd convinced himself it wasn't fair to bring anything up without any solid answers, but now he wasn't so sure he could make it through the night without saying something. His heart was too heavy, and his hand too numb.

"Aarov, I just don't want to go," Leena said stubbornly, standing in the hallway. The twins had just fallen back to sleep, and Leena's parents waited quietly in the other room.

"But they're asleep, and we don't have to stay until midnight—"

"You're not hearing me! I'm exhausted! Paul hasn't been sleeping well, and these two are using up any last ounce of energy I have."

"You're going to go to bed at six-thirty?" Aarov pressed.

Leena crossed her arms over her chest. "You know very well if we go, there's no way we'll get back at a decent time."

"But we have willing babysitters—"

"You think they can handle the twins?" Leena hissed. "They're almost eighty years old, Aarov!"

"Even if they did nothing but make sure the house doesn't burn down, they'd be fine! Most likely, they'll sleep for the next couple of hours anyway."

"And what about Paul?"

"They can handle one child awake, can't they?" he whispered.

Leena groaned in frustration. "I look like a zombie, and none of my clothes fit—the last thing I want is to be seen in public."

"But this isn't public. These are our friends—basically family. It's at Karl and Nicole's, not some uppity place like last year—"

"I didn't have time to make anything—"

"I can bring the bags of chips I bought the other day."

She eyed him suspiciously. "You'd give up your chips?"

"That's how much this party means to me."

"Will you wake up with the kids tonight so I can sleep?"

Aarov hesitated. "I can't really feed the twins—"

Leena moved close, her eyes ablaze. "But you can bring them to me, so I don't have to get up. And you can change their diapers."

"Alright, it's a deal."

Leena grinned smugly. "Give me fifteen minutes."

"Oh, I see, now you suddenly have energy?" Aarov called after her, running his hands through his hair.

*"I haven't had many opportunities to play lately," Leena sighed. "I don't know. I thought I'd become a performer full-time, but it isn't working out." She sighed, stretching out in the hammock they'd tied between the trees.*

*Nicole nodded, prepping dinner at the picnic table with Karl. Glancing over, she found Aarov setting up the propane stove. Feeling slightly guilty, she lowered her feet to the ground and walked over to help.*

*"I've heard you play before," Mike said, stepping out of the tent and slipping his shoes on before walking toward them.*

*"When?" Leena asked, putting a hand on her hip.*

*"Before you and Aarov even got together."*

*Leena looked at her boyfriend.*

*"It's true," Aarov grinned. "Remember that concert I attended? I came up and talked with you after?"*

*Leena nodded.*

*"Karl and Mike were there with me that night."*

*"Why?" she asked.*

*"Because we had to see the girl Aarov kept talking about day and night," Karl teased.*

*"Not all day and night," Aarov muttered.*

*Mike pulled the paper plates and cups from the back of the car. "You were incredible. That quartet number?"*

*"Oh, that was so good," Karl agreed.*

*"I feel a little left out," Nicole said. "How come I've never heard you play?"*

*Leena shrugged, a broad smile on her face.*

"You've got to find a way to do something with your music," Mike said. "Go for the Philharmonic or something."

Leena laughed out loud. "Yeah, I'll just go right on over and audition."

"You should," Mike said, searching for the salt and pepper in their camping bin. "What's the worst that could happen. They say no? You already don't play with the Philharmonic, so it's a no-lose situation."

Leena opened her mouth to say something but then closed it again.

"You're outstanding," Mike reiterated, pulling the shakers free and handing them to Nicole.

Leena sat down at the table and began opening cans of diced tomatoes and corn to speed up the stew making process. Could she —Leena—audition for the Philharmonic?

"Should I open two of these? Are your parents eating with us?" she asked Karl.

He nodded, and she grabbed another can.

AMANDA HELD COLIN'S HAND AS KARL TURNED OFF THE video. He'd waited to turn it on until Aarov and Leena had arrived, and it was worth the wait. She knew it'd been coming since she'd participated in it but didn't realize how many people they'd contacted.

"How did you find his friends from high school to record that?" Victoria asked, wiping a tear from her cheek.

"That was all Nicole. After she had Mike, she spent hours each day tracking down leads," Karl answered. "Wait, nobody get up," he said, running into the other room. He came back with his camera and snapped a picture of the group.

"Seriously?" Leena complained. "At least warn us so we can fix our mascara."

"Sorry," Karl said, setting the camera on his chair.

Nicole picked up where they'd left off. "The people on Facebook were easy, but most of his teachers and coaches weren't on there. I wanted to make sure we allowed everyone an opportunity to remember him."

"Nicole uploaded this on YouTube so anyone can watch it," Karl said proudly. "It already has four thousand views."

"Whoa, four thousand? I guess people need inspiration these days," Aarov said, rubbing Leena's arm next to him.

Amanda sat back and scanned the room. Something was off. Evan sat next to Alexis, technically smiling and joining in on the conversation, but the dark circles under his eyes and the way he held his left hand...had he lost weight since the last time she'd seen him?

Aarov and Leena also had dark circles under their eyes, but they had the best excuse in the world to be exhausted. She hadn't met the twins yet, but she could only imagine what having three kids under three could do to a person's sanity.

Alexis seemed to be mostly herself. More mature, though. Amanda didn't know how she felt about that. With Mike gone, she was desperate for someone in her life to be a little reckless.

Initially, when they'd turned over the lease to their apartment and gone their separate ways, she'd thought it would be a relief. No more mess in the kitchen, no more random people in the living room at all hours of the night. Instead, there'd been no more ridiculous Shopper's runs at midnight, no more Peter's milkshakes on a Saturday afternoon, and no more annoyed rants that always ended up with both of them laughing so hard they had to grab onto something to keep from falling over.

She missed that.

"I'm going to go get a pop. You want one?" Amanda asked, squeezing Colin's hand.

"Hmm?" he asked, looking up from his phone.

She raised an eyebrow, noticing the hockey scores on his screen.

"Do you want anything from the kitchen?" she asked again.

"No, I'm good," he said, flashing a smile of contrition.

Amanda walked toward the counter in the other room. She knew this wasn't precisely Colin's scene, and he had been traveling all morning. Still, she hoped he'd engage with people at some point. He was a therapist, wasn't he? It's not like he lacked interpersonal skills. And he should understand how important it was to her that he get to know her friends.

"Hey stranger," a voice said next to her, and she jumped.

"Evan," she said, almost pityingly. She hadn't meant it to come out that way, but as she looked at his face—

"I haven't met your boyfriend yet," he said, a harmless grin on his lips. "I assume he's a nice guy?"

Amanda smiled back at him. "Yes," she said simply.

"No more details than that?"

She picked up a clear, disposable cup and filled the bottom with ice. "He's a therapist and academic advisor—"

"Scandalous."

"Not my academic advisor, but thanks for that," she teased.

"So I shouldn't say too much around him; that's what I'm hearing from all this."

"Probably smart."

"Though, really, I shouldn't say too much around you these days. Are you well into your Ph.D. at this point?" he asked, leaning against the counter. Though she could tell he'd put product in his hair, it was too long to stay put, making him look slightly wild and unruly. Even with his Oxford shirt.

"I am," she answered, pouring the sparkling soda. "I've started my dissertation."

"Oh yeah? What on?"

"Relationships and grief."

Evan nodded contemplatively. "If you ever need a study subject," he said, smiling ruefully.

"I think we're all perfect subjects in a way," she said gently. "How's Kayla? I'm sure she's doing great things. She seemed very driven." Amanda reached for the bottles of flavoring and the milk.

"She is that. We've both been busy with work. We're most likely being acquired in the next few months."

Amanda lifted her finished French soda to her lips and took a sip. "I'm sorry. I hope it all goes smoothly. And I hope you're happy, Evan," she said, surprising herself. She hadn't meant to get vulnerable.

"Are you?" he asked, looking at her intensely.

"I am," she nodded, glancing at Colin and Victoria in deep conversation.

Evan followed her gaze. "You've always inspired me," he said. "It seems like nothing in life can ever keep you down."

"You haven't seen me when I run out of chocolate," she laughed, unsure how to respond to his compliment.

"That's true," he smiled, letting her off the hook. "I guess a life-threatening car accident and years of rigorous education pale in comparison to that."

Amanda laughed, rubbing her hip without thinking. "It's terrific to see you, Evan."

"You, too," he said softly as she walked past.

"WHERE'S AMY TONIGHT?" MIKE ASKED, SITTING NEXT TO EVAN *on the couch in front of the TV.*

*"Have you showered yet? You reek," Evan said, waving his hand in front of his nose."*

*"I went skiing with Amanda today."*

*"Oh yeah? That explains the smell. How'd it go?"*

*"I kissed her."*

*Evan turned off the TV and turned to him, eyes wide. "No way. When?"*

*"Outside the ski lodge."*

*"And?"*

*"It was amazing. She's such a cool girl. Even though she's a terrible skier—well, I shouldn't say that. She's a lot better after today. Anyway, it was hard for her, but she skied the entire day. Only one stop for lunch and one hot chocolate break. She didn't complain once."*

*"Sounds like a keeper."*

*Mike nodded. "She's funny, crazy smart—did you know she wants to be a therapist?"*

*"Do you have to be smart to be a therapist?" Evan asked.*

*Mike punched his shoulder. "I think it's cool she wants to help people."*

*"It is; I'm kidding," Evan laughed. "Sounds like you're pretty into her."*

*"There just aren't many girls who are up for looking stupid in front of people. I love that," he said nodding. "I think I'm going to*

*invite her to the New Year's party. You and Karl can meet her and tell me what you think."*

*"I'll see if I can find some time to talk with her. Get some insider information."*

*Mike laughed. "You're going to love her. And I'll go shower now. Before I sweat all over the couch."*

*"Gross. Please do."*

*Evan turned the TV back on and stretched out, specifically avoiding the spot where Mike had been sitting a few seconds before.*

## 9

## DECEMBER 31, 2007

Amanda started awake, nearly rolling off the narrow couch in Evan's hospital room. Linda—his mother—had gone to the hotel for the night. They'd been switching off to get some uninterrupted sleep.

Evan moaned, moving his head slightly, and Amanda rushed to his bedside, pulling a chair up to the side of the mattress. He'd been doing that lately. 'A good sign,' the nurse had said earlier in the afternoon. His surgery had been three days ago, but they were taking their time waking him up. Giving him time to heal and recover without the added task of being conscious.

As it turned out, she hadn't been crazy to notice a difference in Evan's appearance a year ago. Though he didn't say anything about it that night, she heard from Nicole only a month later that he was going in for a brain scan. He'd had numbness in his limbs on and off for weeks before he traveled back home, and only weeks after he left, he'd collapsed on the forty-ninth floor of the Bank of America Building just as he passed the main desk.

She'd immediately gotten in touch with Evan's mom

through Nicole, and they'd talked weekly ever since. His first MRI in San Francisco showed potential signs of Tumefactive Multiple Sclerosis. How it was different from regular MS, she had no clue. Except that patients with this type were often misdiagnosed as having brain tumors. When Amanda saw the scans, she remembered thinking she didn't know which team to root for. Cancer vs. MS.

The sale of Evan's company had gone through, and instead of staying on through the merger, he'd quit and moved back to Calgary. Linda wanted a second opinion, and in May, she got it. Another MRI with the same interpretation.

When the medications did nothing to help with his symptoms, they got another scan in October. And then a biopsy. And now, here they were at the Princess Margaret Cancer Foundation in Toronto.

The steady beeps and unpredictable hisses from the machines made Amanda cringe. She leaned forward, resting her elbows on the bed as she checked her messages. Nicole, Alexis, and Victoria had been sending her messages all night. They'd been hesitant at first, but she'd eventually been successful at convincing them that she'd much rather see the fun they were having than imagine it.

Aarov and Leena had come back to Calgary for the holidays. With his new schedule, he often got a few weeks off at a time. The trade-off was living in Fort McMurray, which Leena swore wasn't as bad as it sounded, but Amanda wasn't convinced. Raising four children in ten-months-out-of-the-year-winter sounded like her personal nightmare.

She scrolled through pictures of her friends playing games, eating butter tarts, pretending to be sad they weren't there, drawing motivational cancer slogans on their body parts—Karl in a pink, lacy bra was a highlight she'd be saving for Evan when he woke up.

Colin's face suddenly appeared on her screen, and she picked up.

"Hey," she said softly.

"How're you holding up?"

"Good, I took a nap after dinner."

"Hospital food?"

"Ugh. Absolutely not. I ordered in."

"That's my girl," Colin laughed. "It's almost midnight there, isn't it?"

"In an hour," she yawned.

"Shoot. I miscalculated. Should I ring you back then?"

Amanda grinned. "You can if you want. Or we can just pretend it's midnight now."

"Happy New Year!" he shouted, and she held the phone away from her ear.

"Do you have a noise maker?"

"I picked up a pack of them at the dollar store."

"Impressive. It felt like I was there for a minute," she said blandly.

Colin laughed, blowing it one more time into the speaker.

"I'm sorry I'm not there with you," she sighed. "Thank you for understanding why I needed to come."

Colin was silent for a moment. "I miss you," he said finally.

"I miss you, too. Love you. See you in a couple days."

Amanda hung up the phone and set it on the sheets in front of her.

She sighed, looking at Evan's bandaged head. She could barely see his face with the tubes and bandages, and she wondered if this was what she looked like that night. Probably worse. She'd been bandaged head to toe from what she could remember. But she knew what lay under those bandages in front of her. A handsome face, a bold smile, determined eyes. He had sat in similar circumstances for a perfect stranger.

She reached out and wrapped her hand around his. What had he said to her? She'd kill for a recording of that night.

It wasn't fair that he was here now. Ripped from a job he loved, unsure whether he'd wake up with the same brain capacity as before, not guaranteed to regain full motor function. And that was all before the radiation and chemotherapy started.

He needed to be okay. She closed her eyes, and doubled over, resting her head on the mattress. The nurse had mentioned that it could be comforting to hear people's voices that his brain recognized—that even in this state, there might be times when he could 'hear' them.

The only tune that came to her head was Edelweiss of all things. She closed her eyes and hummed.

## 10

## DECEMBER 31, 2008

Evan brushed his hair back, attempting to make it stay in place. It was thinner now, whether from cancer treatment or getting closer to forty, he couldn't tell. He'd blame cancer treatment all day, though.

"Hey, you ready to go?" Alexis asked, wrapping her arms around his waist from behind.

"I think so," he said, setting down his comb and turning to face her.

She stepped on her tiptoes and kissed him. "You look great."

"I look like I'm malnourished," he laughed.

"Well, you are. We're working on that," she said, tapping his nose. "Have you heard from Aarov?"

"Yeah, they got in before Christmas but won't be there tonight. Paul's throwing up."

A disgusted expression passed over her face. "And that is exactly why I'm never having kids."

Evan laughed. "Doesn't sound like a walk in the park."

"No," she asserted. "All of the body stuff—" she

motioned to her chest and stomach. "That alone is enough to turn me off."

She walked out of the bathroom and lifted her coat from a hanger in the hallway closet.

"You're serious?" Evan asked. "You never want kids?"

"One-hundred percent."

"How did I not know this?" he said, his grin slowly fading.

"With all the chemicals you've had in your body, there's no way you could have kids anyway," she teased, putting the hanger back on the bar.

Evan cleared his throat. "I saved them."

She blinked, slipping into her winter coat. "What do you mean?"

"I mean, we had a meeting before I started my treatment, and they talked about how I'd be sterile afterward. I chose to freeze my...guys. So I could still have that option later."

Alexis stared at him. "Umm, this is a pretty heavy topic right before a party. Maybe we could table it and talk later?"

Evan nodded, reaching for his own coat and following her toward the door.

AMANDA STARED AT THE RING ON HER FINGER, TWISTING IT around and around. It was beautiful. A simple solitaire diamond on a thin, platinum band.

Colin had proposed within a week of her returning from Toronto last year. He'd taken her to Banff; they'd ridden the Gondola and experienced the spectacular view of the Rockies from the top walkways. Then, later that night at dinner in the Banff Springs hotel, he'd popped the question.

She'd said yes without hesitation. Colin was intelligent, ethical, hard-working, and consistent. She knew they'd be able to build a meaningful life together.

Now, that ring had been sitting on her finger for nearly an entire year, and they still hadn't nailed down a date. True, their year hadn't exactly gone as planned. She'd been finishing her Ph.D., and he'd been heading up a monumental study that had experienced significant setbacks. Multiple times. But that didn't mean they couldn't at least start planning—a little.

But she didn't want to bring it up again, not yet. And right now was not the time to go down that rabbit hole.

"Where do you want these?" Colin asked, stepping inside with a handful of Christmas lights.

"Oh, here," she said, pulling a large Tupperware storage container from the hall. "This is for the outdoor lights."

Colin set the strings gently in the bottom, then went back outside to finish the task.

Amanda knew it was early to be taking down her decorations, but it was going to be an insane couple of weeks after this, and a huge blizzard was coming in the next few days; she didn't want to be *that* person who had their lights up until February.

VICTORIA OPENED THE DOOR TO FRIEND AFTER FRIEND, AND her heart felt full for the first time all season. She'd spent over a week setting up her grandmother's Christmas village on the bookshelves, organizing the living area to accommodate everyone, and baking all of her holiday favorites. Every day a new scent had filled the house: homemade Chex mix, gingersnaps, chocolate peanut butter pretzels, and caramel popcorn balls. If she didn't have kids to eat this stuff up, at least she could make it for friends and not get stuck devouring it all herself. Because *not* baking it wasn't an option.

"Looks amazing," Jesse said. And it did. The house dazzled, just as she hoped it would. Twinkle lights strung across the bookshelves gave perfect ambient lighting, white paper snowflakes added whimsy above the buffet, and the live garland along the banister smelled of cinnamon and pine. Which really didn't explain why she wanted to walk to her room and burst into tears.

The evening progressed as so many parties had in the past; Victoria shuffled around the room catching up on everyone's lives, they played games, and ate until they had zero desire to fill their plates again. At least for the moment. Smiles, laughter, gasps of surprise, and then this. Victoria standing with Amanda in the kitchen, talking as she refilled the charcuterie platter.

"When did you and Jesse set a date?" Amanda asked, watching her as she pulled a package of salami from the fridge.

"For the wedding? Oh, pretty much immediately. Well, I guess that's overstating it. He proposed, and it would've been...about three months later, I think? We started researching venues and finally settled on one."

Amanda nodded introspectively. "It's been almost a year," she said slowly.

"Since you got engaged?" Victoria asked, making a line on the white plate with the circles of meat.

Snitching a piece of salami from the package, Amanda nodded. "Do you think it means something?"

"Like what?"

"I don't know. Maybe he doesn't actually want to get

married?" she said, leaning in toward her like she was sharing a dirty secret.

"Well, he proposed, didn't he? Seems like that means he's invested."

"I know," Amanda said, taking a deep breath. "But I kind of pushed for it."

"How so?" Victoria turned to put the package back in the fridge and pulled out a Ziploc bag of cheese she'd pre-sliced that afternoon.

"I talked about it a lot. Told him I wanted to get married before I turned forty. Talked about wanting to start a family and all that."

"Were those things true?"

"Still are."

"Then you can't apologize for it. Either you have the same goals or you don't, it's as simple as that."

"Is it, though? Aren't relationships about compromise?"

Victoria laughed derisively. "Compromise is great and all, but you can only give so much. If your goals are completely opposite to his, then neither of you are going to be happy. You'll end up in some miserable middle ground. And trust me, life will throw enough curveballs at you that you're going to need him in your corner. At least for the important stuff."

Amanda paused. "Are you and Jesse doing okay?"

That was the question. The question that undid all of the walls she'd built around her heart, specifically for tonight. As soon as the words left Amanda's lips, Victoria began to crumble.

"Our relationship's great—" Victoria started weakly, but couldn't get anything else out. Pursing her lips, she attempted to reign in her emotions, but couldn't. Tears pooled in her eyes, and she began to sob.

Amanda darted around the edge of the counter and pulled her into a hug. She couldn't even begin to form coherent sentences, her emotions were too close to the surface. Amanda held her tightly, not saying a word.

A few minutes later, the flood of emotions retreated slightly, and Victoria lifted her head from Amanda's shoulder.

"Our relationship is great," she repeated, wiping her eyes. "But we've been trying to get pregnant for over a year now."

"I had no idea," Amanda said.

Victoria sniffed. "I know a year isn't the end of the world."

"No, that's a long time to be trying and waiting. I'm so sorry."

"It's just so scary, you know? What if we won't *ever* be able to have kids. And I know there are other options, like adoption, but that's terrifying, too. You hear about people adopting and having tons of issues or having to give their baby back. All of it sounds so draining and difficult."

"To be fair, pushing a human out of your body doesn't sound simple to me either," Amanda grinned.

Victoria laughed, grabbing a tissue from the counter and blowing her nose. "I think the difference is that at least I'm somewhat in control of that. Or at least it seems that way."

Amanda sighed, leaning back against the counter. "What are you going to do?"

"Well, now that we've been trying for this long with no results, our doctor is willing to do some testing. So that's good news. I've got an appointment for both of us mid-January."

"That's great. Maybe it will be an easy fix."

"Fingers crossed." She took a deep breath. "Are you going to be okay?"

"Me?"

"Yeah, with the whole wedding thing."

Amanda laughed. "Oh yeah. That." She stood up straight. "I don't know. I'm sure we'll figure it out. Would you mind if I went outside to get some air?"

"Of course," Victoria nodded. "If you go into the dining room, there's a door that leads onto the balcony."

"Thanks. I'm sure I'm making a bigger deal of this than it really is."

Victoria watched her leave the kitchen, then picked up the platter and followed.

AMANDA COUGHED SLIGHTLY AS SHE TOOK HER FIRST BREATH of the frigid winter air. She'd gotten slightly overheated inside with her thick sweater on. She knew she wouldn't last long out here, but for now, it felt glorious.

"Another escapee?" a voice said next to her, and she gasped.

"Evan," she breathed. "You scared me."

He grinned. "Sorry."

"You were smart," she said, noticing his winter coat.

"I haven't gained enough weight back yet to regulate my temperature consistently," he said.

Amanda's heart dropped. She'd noticed how different he looked, but it was easier to disregard when he wasn't directly commenting on it.

"So what brings you to the chilly December air this evening?" he asked with mock formality.

"Nothing really, just needed a moment to think."

"Am I ruining it?"

"No," she smiled. "Besides, you were here first."

"Right. You're ruining my moment. Glad you recognized that."

Amanda laughed, leaning on the railing and looking up at the stars. She drew in a breath sharply. "Look!"

Evan walked closer to her. She pointed at a slight glimmer of neon green visible between the houses.

"I haven't seen the northern lights since I was a kid," he breathed.

"Probably because we're always inside at night in the winter now. I used to go outside in the cold and dark all the time when I was younger."

"Night games," he grinned.

"Sledding for me."

He sighed. "I haven't gone sledding in forever."

"Should we go?" Amanda said suddenly.

Evan looked at her, his interest piqued. "Now?"

"Why not? We always play games at these parties. What if we did that instead?"

"I would totally do it..."

"But?"

"I don't know if I'll be able to convince Alexis. She hates the snow. Especially after living south of the border."

Amanda took a deep breath. It was true. And she doubted Colin would be game either.

"It's a great idea, though," he said, nudging her arm with his. "Remember when we all used to be more spontaneous?"

She nodded. "I remember when I was. I didn't know all of you before everyone started to settle down."

"True," he grinned. "I wish you had. It was pretty epic."

"I could see Karl being pretty crazy in college."

"I had to reign him in," Evan laughed.

Amanda pulled her hands inside her sleeves, beginning

to shiver. She took a deep breath and let it out slowly. "Is this where you thought you'd be in 2008?"

"No way!" Evan exclaimed. "I have way less body mass and way more money than I anticipated."

Amanda snorted and laughed out loud, taking a solid minute to compose herself. "The hilarious thing is, I'm exactly where I thought I'd be. I completed the degrees I wanted; I'm beginning to practice the way I always wanted, I'm in a committed relationship..."

"And?" Evan probed.

"And it feels like a life that isn't quite mine yet," she said, her eyebrows furrowing. "Like I'm missing some really important piece that would make sense of all the rest."

Evan was silent next to her. She watched the wisps of color dancing against the inky night sky of the horizon.

"I don't know. Maybe I'm just in a funk." She stood up and rubbed her arms, her teeth beginning to chatter. "I'm going to head inside. Thanks for listening."

"Anytime," he said as she opened the door.

"Karl?" Nicole called down the hall. "Karl, I—what are you doing?" she asked, walking into the den to find him sitting in front of his computer.

"Hey," he said, spinning on his chair, "I was just looking at different lease options for the practice."

"We're supposed to be leaving," she said, switching four-year-old Mike to the other hip, moving around her protruding belly. "I've been working for the last hour to prepare everything so we can go, and you've been in here looking up things for your practice?"

Karl nodded uneasily. "A few places popped up the other day, and I didn't have a chance to look at them then—"

"So you thought crunch time before our babysitter got here was the time to do that?"

Karl stared at her blankly.

"You had all morning to workout and do what you wanted, and I've been cleaning and cooking and trying to take care of the baby, and somehow get dressed during all that—"

"Why didn't you ask for help?"

Nicole's face flushed. "Why is it *my* responsibility to ask for help? Why are these tasks only mine? *You're willing to assist if I ask?* It's not my job to clean our house alone. It's not my job to take care of *our* baby on my own. The butter tarts are kind of my job because I started that tradition, but everything else? *How is that my job, Karl!?*"

Karl turned off the computer and stood up. "I'm trying to do my part to contribute to this family. I've done the work to be able to practice as a dentist, I'm doing everything I can to set up my own practice so I don't have to keep working a terrible schedule under someone else—and all of that is really stressful, by the way—"

"Karl, I'm working in my own business, too! It's stressful to find clients and get our kitchen certified, and figure out the marketing and everything else. We're both working stressful jobs. And I worked so you *could* get that education, and none of this even matters right now, because the babysitter is going to be here any second," Nicole said in a huff, spinning on her heel and walking back to the kitchen.

"Do you want anything else to eat?" she asked Mike, setting him down on his booster seat. He shook his head and picked up his water cup. She took his dishes to the sink, washed them off, and put them in the dishwasher.

The doorbell rang, and she let Karl answer it. Jenny walked into the kitchen a few moments later.

"Hey," Nicole said, drying her hands on the towel. "I already fed him dinner, so you can really just play and get him into bed at his regular time."

Jenny nodded.

"It's going to be a late one, so don't worry if you fall asleep," she said, smiling.

"I stay up that late all the time," Jenny scoffed. "I'll be fine."

"Well, thanks for giving up your New Year's Eve so we can go out."

Jenny smiled and Karl appeared in the archway. Nicole turned and kissed Mike's cheek. "See you soon, buddy," she said, then followed Karl into the hall to get her coat.

"I'M NOT GOING TONIGHT," ALEXIS SAID, STRETCHING OUT ON the couch, holding the phone to her ear.

"But I haven't seen you in so long, and I'm hosting," Victoria whined on the other end.

"Taylor's coming over, and we're going to watch a movie."

"Are you guys dating?"

"Maybe. Maybe not."

"Why don't you bring him? He's been to one of our parties before."

"Yeah, because that wouldn't be awkward. Me seeing Evan and Taylor seeing Amanda?"

"You and Evan being in the same room is going to be awkward whenever you see each other next, so why put it off? And I highly doubt Taylor would care about seeing Amanda. They were faking it anyway."

"But Evan didn't know that at the time."

Victoria laughed. "Very true. You didn't ever tell him when you were together?"

"No, why would I?"

"You're getting me off-topic. Back to the issue of you not coming to the party—"

"You're not going to convince me! The literal last thing I want to do right now is see Evan."

"You still haven't told me what happened between you."

"Because it's none of your business."

"Okay, ouch."

"I didn't mean it like that," Alexis sighed. "I think I need more time before I rehash it."

"I get it. And I really don't need to know details; it just makes me sad that it was apparently bad enough that you're uncomfortable coming. We've had this tradition going for ten years!"

"Well, maybe it's time for it to be over," Alexis said. "I don't mean to sound heartless, but we're all at different points now. Those friendships are an important part of my life, but maybe I need to move on. Not be defined by who I was then, eh?"

Victoria was silent for a moment. "I think we're all moving on in our own ways, but I still think this connection is important."

"You've always been more nostalgic than me."

"It's true." Alexis took a deep breath. "I'm really not going to be able to convince you?"

"No, sorry."

"Can we get together tomorrow? Our office is closed until the third."

"When do you and Jesse start with Karl, by the way?"

"Not until March at the earliest. He hasn't found a lease yet. Then we have to do the build-out."

"Can I be your first patient in the new office?"

"I'm counting on it."

"I'm not paying."

Victoria laughed. "Tomorrow?"

"I'll phone you when I wake up."

❊

"THANKS FOR DRIVING ALL THE WAY OUT HERE AGAIN," Victoria smiled, hugging Karl and Nicole.

"They need to hurry up and move to Calgary," Aarov said from the couch.

"Whatever," Karl laughed. "Now that we have CrossIron Mills, we don't need to come into Calgary for anything."

"Where is your practice going to be?" Leena asked as they were hanging up their coats.

"Not sure yet," Karl said, avoiding Nicole's gaze. "I'm looking at the new developments on the west side of Airdrie but haven't found the perfect spot yet."

"You two are going to commute?" Aarov asked. "What is that, thirty-five minutes or so?"

"Yeah," Victoria said, looking at Jesse. "We haven't fully decided yet. We might consider moving out there to be closer."

Aarov threw up his hands.

"You can't say anything, man. You live in Fort Mac!"

"I had no real choice in the matter," he laughed. "But, I think we'll be coming back in the summer."

"Really?" Nicole said excitedly. "That's fantastic!"

"We're hoping it all works out," Leena said. "But I think we're going to have to buy a bigger house. We saved up some money renting out the top floor of our other one; it's just too small with all the kids now."

"Your parents are still living downstairs?" Victoria asked, and Leena nodded.

"I hear Airdrie is a good place to look," Karl teased.

The door opened behind them, and Amanda and Colin walked in. Victoria watched her pause as she noticed the pile of snow boots on the entry mat. Amanda looked up and scanned the room.

"Did none of you decide to dress up this year?" she

asked. "Not that I'm complaining; I think it's great that you've all sunk to my casual level."

Victoria fought back a laugh. "I wasn't in the mood to be fancy, I guess," she said simply. The others nodded in agreement.

Amanda's eyes narrowed, but she didn't comment. Instead, she walked into the room and greeted everyone with a hug, then sat down on the loveseat and waited for Colin to join her.

EVAN WAITED IN HIS CAR WITH THE ENGINE OFF. WHEN HE SAW Amanda arrive, his heart bubbled up with childlike excitement. He knew this could be a terrible idea. But that's why it was so enticing.

When she shut the door to the house, he quickly stepped to the street and began unloading the toboggans two at a time, stacking them next to Victoria's garage. They were cheap, $10 sleds from Co-op, but he didn't care if they lasted longer than tonight. A few runs down the massive hill at the other end of the cul-de-sac was all they needed.

He pulled on a toque, grabbed his gloves from the car, and stood on the walkway a moment. Something had changed within him this past year. Two years. Almost dying tends to do that to a person. Prior to his diagnosis, he'd been on a different track. A path of building wealth, convincing everyone—including himself—that he had everything together, and climbing the corporate ladder. Now, the sheer knowledge that any day living a somewhat average life could be his last made it impossible to be motivated by all that.

That's why he couldn't stay with Alexis. He knew she thought he'd judged her reasoning unfairly, and maybe he had. She was one of the most giving people he'd ever met. Her selfless work with her various non-profits proved that well enough. And they had so much in common there. He wanted to do good in the world and contribute in meaningful ways. It's just that he wanted a family to be part of the equation.

Figuring he'd given Amanda enough time to settle in, he walked toward the front door.

"Ho, ho, ho!" he called dramatically as he waltzed into the house.

Everyone turned their heads, and Nicole beamed at him.

"If you would all kindly get your coats and boots on and follow me outside, I'd greatly appreciate it," he said with mock formality.

The group obediently stood, but Amanda looked back and forth in confusion. "What are we doing?"

"You'll see," Evan said, grinning widely.

"I have boots for you two if you didn't wear appropriate footwear," Victoria smiled. "And plenty of extra toques and gloves."

Amanda stood and followed Aarov and Leena toward the door. She took Victoria up on her extra winter wear, as did Colin. When everyone was dressed, they walked out onto the driveway.

Evan was already there and handed everyone their own sled.

Amanda laughed out loud. Staring at him in amazement, she walked closer to retrieve her toboggan. "You remembered?" she asked quietly.

"I thought it'd be fun. Especially when Victoria told me she had an amazing sledding hill right here on her street."

"You were in on this?" she said, wheeling on Victoria.

She nodded. "We kind of all were."

Evan watched Amanda's face. Her eyes sparkled with amusement. He knew she was getting married, and he wasn't in any way trying to undermine her relationship with Colin; he seemed like a nice enough guy, even if he was a little serious. No, he just loved making her smile. That was it.

"Follow me!" Victoria called, walking briskly down the sidewalk with Jesse in tow.

In less than a minute, they found themselves at the top of a path that led between the homes and into a green space. Rather, a black and white space at this time of night. One street lamp illuminated the hill, and Amanda ran past the group in excitement. Without hesitating, she jumped onto her sled mid-step and sailed down the snowbank.

The rest of the group quickly followed—Karl had gone back for his camera—and within moments, Karl was back snapping pictures of all nine of them covered in snow and laughing hysterically.

Aarov pushed Leena over as he raced back to the top of the hill. Evan immediately gave chase, breathing hard as he ran him down. When Evan finally reached the top, Aarov was already on his toboggan, pushing off with his hands to escape. Evan barreled toward him and launched himself onto Aarov's sled, nearly toppling them both. Aarov swiped at him, but Evan wrapped his feet around his waist and they shot down the hill, curving to the left, nearly running into Jesse.

Immediately, the girls—except Nicole with her extra cargo—tried to outdo them and all jump on the same sled together. Victoria stretched herself across their laps and only made it halfway down before being tossed into the snow. The sled came to an erratic and unexpected stop, and the women collapsed sideways into a heap of laughter.

"I'm about done," Colin called from the path, and Amanda waved him back to the house. "Where would you like the sled, mate?" Colin asked as he passed.

"Just stack it against the garage. Thanks for being a good sport," Evan smiled.

"I'll come with you!" Jesse called from halfway down the hill. Grabbing his sled, he ran to meet him at the top. "My jeans are already soaked through," he said breathlessly. "I've never been so grateful that Victoria offered to host."

"We're having a competition!" Aarov yelled loudly across the hill. "Who can go the furthest—single rider!"

The girls brushed off their pants and ran up to join in the fun. Based on mass and potential energy alone, they knew their chances of winning were slim, but they immediately began strategizing. Evan didn't think he'd have a shot, though he had been trying to bulk up over the past year.

Karl and Aarov beat them all by a couple of feet.

"I'm definitely a few inches in front of you!" Aarov exclaimed, drawing an imaginary line from the toe of his boot across the snow.

"Whatever!" Karl laughed. "Look at this!" he said, standing carefully and walking in a straight line from where his boot hit the snow at the front of his sled.

"You're walking diagonally!" Aarov argued, laughing and throwing a snowball at his friend.

"I declare a tie!" Nicole called from behind them. "Don't kill each other!"

Eventually, their pants began to freeze, and they collectively decided it wouldn't be wise to end the night with pneumonia. Pulling their sleds, they ran back to the house.

"Do you want me to help you put these in your car?" Amanda asked Evan as they brushed the snow off the cold plastic with their gloves.

"No," he laughed. "I wasn't planning on taking them home. I figured I could leave them out for neighborhood kids or something."

"Here, I've got an idea," she grinned, her eyes lighting up. She ran inside with the others and returned a few minutes later with paper, tape, and a Sharpie.

"Turn around," she commanded, and Evan obeyed. Amanda pressed the paper against his back, and he could feel her writing something.

"There," she said proudly.

Evan turned and saw a large 'FREE' written across the white surface. She taped it to the stack of sleds and dragged them to the sidewalk.

"Love it," Evan said. He watched her adjust the positioning of the sleds, her dirty blond hair spilling out from under her toque and her breath billowing up in clouds.

"The kids'll be thrilled," she said, turning and walking up the driveway. She stopped in front of him and met his eyes. "Thank you, Evan," she said gently, her smile stretching from ear to ear. "This is the highlight of my year."

"Mine, too," he breathed as she passed him and walked back into the house.


"Hey," Karl said, reaching out to his wife, her hair slightly curly and wet from the snow. "I'm really sorry about earlier."

"I'm sorry, too. I was stressed and—"

"I appreciate your apology, but I think you were right," he said, putting an arm around Nicole's shoulder.

She looked up at him, surprised. "I'm excited to hear where this is headed."

"I need to take more responsibility at home, especially

with our family growing. Maybe we can sit down and figure out how I can be most helpful."

Nicole smiled. "I'd love that. This feels like Christmas all over again."

"Don't get too excited," Karl laughed. "I'm talking unloading the dishwasher, sweeping. You know, mindless stuff."

Nicole elbowed him lightly in the ribs. "We'll see about that. You've opened Pandora's box now."

Karl grabbed her hand, and she led him back into the living room.

"IVF, SO FUN RIGHT NOW," VICTORIA SAID WITH A CAUSTIC laugh.

The group sat on the rug around the fireplace, cuddled in blankets, outfitted in Victoria and Jesse's extra sweats and wool socks.

"I'm so sorry you've had to deal with all that," Amanda said. "When do you find out whether it took?"

"Another few weeks. I'll keep you guys posted. I'm praying it works because I don't know if I can go through that whole process again."

"I've heard it's brutal," Leena said. "We're all rooting for you."

"If it doesn't work, maybe Nicole could be your surrogate," Karl said, nudging his wife.

"Ummm, hello? I'm already baking one at the moment," she said, motioning to her belly.

"I meant after," Karl said, and Nicole elbowed him.

"I'm just hoping my eggs are even viable. I'm getting old enough that even surrogacy might be a stretch," Victoria laughed.

Amanda looked down at her lap uncomfortably, and Victoria noticed.

"I'm kidding," Victoria said warmly. "We've all still got plenty of time left."

"No, I know," Amanda said, fiddling with her engagement ring.

"I figure if kids happen, great. If not, it wasn't meant to be," Colin said, rubbing Amanda's shoulder. "Sometimes I wonder if my mentoring is better suited to patients and students anyway. I've alway been rubbish with small children."

"When have you spent time with small children?" Amanda asked, her brow furrowed.

"Just nieces and nephews, my sister's kids."

"They still live in England. You've seen them, what— once in the last five years?" she pressed.

"Well, I think it's been more often than that," he hedged, shifting uncomfortably.

Amanda sighed and turned her gaze back to the dancing flames over the grate.

"I've never been good with small kids either," Aarov piped in compassionately. "Until I had my own kids. It's different when they're yours."

"That's what I've heard," Colin said. "I'm not sure the research supports that, though."

Aarov nodded. "It felt different for me."

"I'm sure it does feel different, but the actual translation of skill is more my concern. I don't relish the thought of passing down my own bad habits and dysfunction to the next generation, eh?" he laughed uncomfortably.

"So you think only perfect people have a right to be parents?" Amanda said softly.

"Not a 'right,' but we have a social responsibility to be

prudent, don't you think? Only create what we can provide for physically and emotionally?"

"Sure," Leena jumped in, "but who's to say what each child needs exactly? I know for us, each kid is so different. I might be a perfect parent for one, but all of them? Seems unlikely."

Colin nodded, chewing on this comment.

"If there had been any sort of vetting procedure, we wouldn't have gotten the job," Karl laughed. "Or at least I wouldn't have. Nicole's got it down."

Nicole raised an eyebrow. "Good save."

"Hey!" Victoria exclaimed. "I need to bring out some treats before our countdown." She jumped to her feet and ran into the kitchen, and Amanda stood up to help.

"It's alright," Evan said, placing a hand lightly on her shoulder. "I've got it."

They returned with plates in both hands and set them in the center of their haphazard circle, and it didn't take long for people to partake.

"Here's to another three-hundred-and-sixty-five days around the sun," Karl said.

"And here's to progress and growth in 2010," Nicole added.

"Here's to Mike," Evan said, holding up a cookie.

"I can't say anything to compete with that," Aarov scoffed. "Way to shut down the toasts."

Evan laughed and shrugged his shoulders.

Victoria grinned, subconsciously holding a hand to her midsection. Would she be a good parent? She had no clue. But she hoped beyond all hope that in 2010 she'd get to try.

## 12

## DECEMBER 31, 2010

"We know where we need to focus this year," Taylor said, leaning forward in his seat. "The statistics are clear. We're losing these kids from Southeast Asia. Graduation rates dropped a full percentage point over the last three years."

The sports bar was packed to the gills. It was only five-thirty, and already people were settling in for the night.

"Not to mention the fact that overall resettlement from that region increased by three percentage points," Alexis added, talking loudly over the din.

Taylor nodded. "I know tonight isn't about work, and I'm not going to harp on it, but when I saw those reports..." he sighed. "I think we need someone on the ground over there to understand the culture better."

"Do you think we'd have enough support for that? Or should we look into recruiting someone who's already experienced into our office for guidance?"

"Not a bad idea..." he mused.

"Even better?" she grinned, excitement in her eyes. "Why don't we pay one of our graduates to consult?"

Taylor's eyes lit up. "Brilliant. As always."

"But," she said, grinning mischievously, "we also need to go to Thailand. For research purposes, of course."

Taylor laughed. "I've got savings. And we have plenty of volunteers lined up for February and March."

"You think we should go for two months?" Alexis raised an eyebrow.

"Don't tempt me."

Alexis reached across the table and squeezed his hand. "I'm going to go to my New Year's Party tonight. I'm sorry I can't stay until everyone else gets here."

"I'll survive. I got you last year. I guess it's only fair," he grinned, leaning over to kiss her cheek. "Love you."

"Love you, too," Alexis said, pulling on her coat and slinging her purse over her shoulder.

"Say hi to Amanda for me."

Alexis groaned, smacking his arm playfully as she walked by.

Amanda walked into her room, her heart hammering wildly in her chest. She couldn't remember why she'd come in here. What was she looking for? Lip gloss. Right. She searched her nightstand, coming up empty. Next, she checked her purse and found it tucked inside her zipper pocket.

She needed to find a way to calm down. There was still an hour before she needed to leave, and she was going to sweat through her shirt by then if something didn't change drastically.

Pulling out her phone, she turned on her chill playlist and walked into the bathroom.

❄

"BROOKE'S ASLEEP," NICOLE SAID.

"I'll go read with Mike," Karl said, stepping away from the empty sink.

"Thanks for doing the dishes. I'm going to make the deviled eggs, and then I think we're ready. We told people six-thirty, right?"

Karl nodded, then dried his hands on a towel and slipped his hand around her waist, pulling her close. "Happy New Year," he whispered, swaying gently.

"Do you get to say that yet?" she smirked.

He chuckled. "I know I haven't been easy to deal with this year."

Nicole inspected his face. His eyes looked tired—weighed down with cares he wouldn't verbalize. It seemed that every year he retreated a little more into his own head. Without inviting her along.

"The past few years, I've just felt—scared," he said softly.

"Of what?" Nicole asked, treading carefully. Terrified she might do or say something that would plug this sudden conduit to his inner thoughts.

Karl took a deep breath. "Of being out of control. Mike's getting older, and he's already becoming super independent. And now Brooke...I'm worried we won't be able to keep them safe."

"We can't, not forever," Nicole said with a smile.

"I haven't come to terms with that yet."

Nicole brushed her fingers over his cheek. "The long hours you're pulling, the intense workouts—is that what this is about?" She paused, lifting up the front of his shirt. "I'm not complaining," she said with a grin, "but don't you think you're running yourself a bit ragged?"

"I don't know what else to do," he breathed. "Another year comes and goes, and it feels like I'm always moving closer to another thing that's going to hurt."

Nicole laid her head against his chest and listened to his heartbeat. "I think life just hurts sometimes."

"I don't want it to."

"I know," she sighed, feeling his hands on her waist and the warmth of his breath on her temple. "We can't keep fighting it, Karl. We need to live fully again. Together."

"I'm not sure I know how."

"Well, I do," she said, lifting her head and meeting his eyes. "We open our hearts. And if they get trampled on, we mend them. Together. We need each other fully. And if we're connected, it doesn't matter what happens. We've made it through loss before, and we can do it again. We can do being poor; we can do being sad, and we can do stress— we've proven that already."

"I just don't want to ever hurt like I did when Mike—" his voice catching.

"The hurt is equivalent to how much you cared. Are you willing to give up that depth of love the rest of your life to avoid any pain? Is that worth it?"

Karl stared at the floor, his brow furrowed. "Have I been doing that?" he asked soberly.

Nicole nodded. "It's like you're here," she said, motioning with her hands, "only living from here on up."

"I'm going to try," he said, clearing his throat. "I want to try."

Nicole smiled and stepped on her tiptoes to kiss his cheek. "I'm glad. I've missed you."

❄

VICTORIA SAT IN THE ROCKING CHAIR, PRESSING HER THREE-and-a-half month old baby girl to her chest. She inhaled deeply, the smell of newness mixed with lavender filling her nostrils. Her heart felt as if it might burst, and she had to actively remember not to squeeze too hard as she rocked.

"Don't we need to leave soon if we're going to make it to Airdrie by six-thirty?" Jesse asked quietly, leaning his head into the nursery.

"But she's so peaceful," she grinned, kissing the top of Phoebe's head.

Jesse walked into the dark room and kneeled next to the chair. "We could just stay home. I could keep both of you to myself."

Victoria sighed. "Don't tempt me."

"I'll go grab the car seat," Jesse said.

"PAUL! STOP TAKING THAT FROM YOUR SISTER!" LEENA YELLED, chasing her five-year-old through the kitchen. She yelped as her foot caught the edge of a stack of boxes against the wall. "Aarov, can you *please* move these into the garage?"

"Right now? Aren't we leaving?"

"DOES IT LOOK LIKE WE'RE LEAVING!?" Leena grabbed Paul's sleeve and pulled a rubber giraffe from his grip. Giving him a stern look, she marched back into the living room and put it back in Ally's outstretched hands.

A clatter sounded from the kitchen and she took a deep breath, turning to investigate. The twins sat in the corner, pulling metal bowls from the cupboard, smashing them together and laughing with delight.

"Where are my parents?" Leena hissed under her breath.

"Aarov, I need you to run out back and tell my parents we need to go."

"They said they were just finishing dinner five minutes ago," he called from their bedroom.

"That means they're probably taking their time doing the dishes; please go remind them we're going to be late!"

"Okay, give me a minute."

Leena pursed her lips. "Here," she said, pulling the twins into the other room. "Play with these." She pulled out a box of wooden blocks.

Paul ran back into the room and jumped on his mother's back, nearly knocking her to the floor.

"Paul, hey," she said, righting herself. "You can't jump on Mommy's back like that, okay? That hurts."

"I love you, Mommy," he said, throwing his arms around her neck and burying his face in her long, black hair. "Don't go."

"I love you, too. And we are going to go."

Paul looked at her, tears forming in the corners of his eyes.

"Nani's going to read to you tonight, okay?"

As if on cue, Leena's parents walked through the front door.

"Finally," Leena breathed, then smiled at Paul. "See? You're going to have a wonderful time."

Paul's lower lip trembled, and he let out a wail. "But I miss our old house, and I don't like my new bedroom and—"

"Paul," Leena said, pulling him toward her and looking at his face, screwed up with emotion. "I know it's hard moving here, but now we get to be next to Nani and Nana again. And I promise we'll get your room decorated and painted before you go back to school." She looked at her mother with pleading eyes.

Her parents slipped off their shoes and walked into the room. Under her arm, Leena's mother carried two children's books, and—without saying a word—she showed them to Paul.

Wiping his nose, Paul looked with interest at the covers.

Aarov finally made an appearance, walking into the room wearing dark jeans, a freshly pressed shirt, and neatly combed hair.

"I'm ready," he said proudly.

Leena rolled her eyes. "Love you," she said, kissing both parents on the forehead and following Aarov out the door to the car.

AMANDA SAT IN NICOLE AND KARL'S LIVING ROOM, ADMIRING their new home. It seemed every one of her friends was upleveling in some way—settling into their long-term homes and businesses, enjoying their stable relationships. This wasn't the first time she sat wondering what on earth she was doing wrong.

She forced her knee to stay still as she dipped her tortilla chips into seven-layer dip, her eyes flicking toward the door every few minutes. It was already seven forty-five. Where was he?

"I have new games for us this year," Nicole said, holding up a stack of paper and a handful of pens. "Get the snacks you want, use the bathroom, and meet back here in ten."

Obediently, half the members of the group stood up. Amanda stayed in her seat. "Aren't we waiting for Evan?" she asked nonchalantly.

"I'm not sure," Nicole said. "He texted Karl earlier and said he might not be able to make it."

Amanda's heart dropped. "Why not?" she asked.

"He said he was exhausted. I guess he didn't get much of a break over Christmas and had some things come up with work yesterday. Karl?" she called as he walked back into the room. "Where did Evan say he was last week?"

"Dubai," he said, sitting down with his now full plate.

"Wow, I didn't realize he was traveling this time of year," Amanda said. "I talked with him a few weeks ago, and he didn't mention it."

Thoughts spun in her head. Had she been imagining their increased closeness over the past months? Ever since she'd ended things with Colin in the spring, they'd been texting. Sometimes late into the night. Why hadn't he told her that he wouldn't be here tonight? Or that he was spending Christmas halfway across the world?

"I think it was pretty spur of the moment," Karl said, taking a bite of quiche.

Not an excuse, she silently thought. *This* is exactly what she'd been mulling over. What was she doing wrong? How was it that she was so inept at reading cues or understanding other people's intentions and feelings? She plastered a smile to her face and leaned back in her seat, trying not to let her disappointment show.

AAROV WATCHED LEENA FILL UP HER CUP WITH WATER. SHE still hadn't said more than a few words to him, and he knew he needed to fix it, but didn't quite know how.

"Can I help you with that?" he asked, reaching out to hold her cup while she scooped dip onto her plate.

"I'm fine, thank you," she said coldly.

"Leena, can we talk a moment?" he said softly, motioning toward the table away from the food line.

She sighed but picked up her plate and cup and followed him.

"I know you're mad at me, and...I know it's because you were busy getting everything ready, and I wasn't helping."

Leena nodded, still not meeting his eyes.

"But you know what it was like in your household growing up," he said. "Did your father help with anything around the house? Mine certainly didn't. He got home from work and my mother waited on him hand and foot."

Leena raised an eyebrow, and Aarov held up his hands in defense.

"I'm not saying that was a good system; I'm simply acknowledging the fact that I don't really know any different. I didn't know I should be helping with those sorts of things because—"

"They're women's work?"

"I don't think they are, but—I guess I did kind of think they were," he admitted. "But now that I'm thinking about it, it doesn't seem fair for you to have to work all day and then keep working while I get a break."

"And Aarov, it's not like I don't want you to have a break. I get breaks sometimes during the day—not often anymore —but I know they'll come again. It's not that. But I want to feel like I have a partner. So I don't have to do all of that alone."

Aarov nodded. "I'm willing to try something different. I think it would be good for me to be more involved with the kids."

Leena smiled. "Thank you," she said, hugging him. "I'm sorry I wasn't speaking to you."

"I really don't like that," Aarov said.

"You don't like it when I talk too much, either."

Aarov's eyes widened slightly.

"So which is it?" Leena asked, and Aarov wasn't quite sure whether she was serious or not. He didn't want to chance it.

"In the middle?" he answered hesitantly.

Leena laughed out loud, grabbing his hand. "I'm teasing; let's go play Nicole's game."

Aarov wiped his brow, allowing her to lead him through the kitchen and into the living room.


"ARE YOU OKAY?" NICOLE ASKED, SETTING THE PAPER AND PENS around the coffee table.

"Yeah," Amanda sighed. "I'm going to go get some food. Sorry, I know I'm probably past the time limit."

Nicole waved her off, but Amanda wasn't watching. She walked into the kitchen with a lump in her throat. This was ridiculous. It was laughable that she'd gotten all worked up about seeing him without even actually knowing whether he felt the same way. Yes, they had a history, but maybe that's what had blinded her.

She'd never been able to let him go fully. Even when they were both happily in other relationships, it's like she'd taken those memories and feelings and packed them carefully in a box, wrapped them with a ribbon, and tucked them away only to self-indulgently sneak peeks every once in a while.

She absently put food onto her plate, barely noticing what she was choosing. Why was she still hanging onto this? For all she knew, he'd buried those feelings a long time ago and only considered her a friend. *That* would make sense of their interactions just as well as him being interested.

They were both alone at the moment; they knew each other well enough to look out for each other, they had good communication skills—their texting was most likely an easy fit for validation and digital companionship. That's it.

But even as she thought it, she couldn't convince herself of it's truthfulness. Her body refused to forget how it felt to be with him, no matter how hard she tried. She'd analyzed more dreams than she could count—even when she was engaged to Colin—trying to understand why he kept showing up.

And now that they were both in the same city, both unattached, both independent and somewhat stable, he *still* wasn't making an effort to choose her.

She needed to burn the box with the ribbon.

"Are you finished with the olives?" a voice sounded next to her.

She blinked. How long had she been standing here? Turning, she opened her mouth to speak and then shut it again.

"Hey," Evan said, reaching past her to pick up the tongs.

"Nicole said you probably weren't coming," Amanda exhaled.

"I took a nap this afternoon."

His arm brushed her shoulder, and her heart began beating so intensely in her chest she could barely breathe.

Putting the tongs down and setting his plate on the counter, he turned to her. She scanned the kitchen and found it empty. *How long had she been standing there?*

Waves of frustration, confusion, longing, and grief washed over her. Combined with the hours of anticipation and anxiety before she arrived, it was all too much for her to handle. Her hands started to shake, her cheeks flushed, and her face contorted as tears formed in her eyes. She quickly spun to face the back wall, gasping for air.

"Hey," Evan said with concern in his voice as he put a hand on her shoulder.

"No," she said quickly, shrugging him off. "Don't be nice to me."

"I don't—"

"You don't get to be nice to me!" she spat, spinning around to face him. "I thought we—" she said, sucking in a breath. "I can't do this anymore, Evan."

"What are you talking about?" he said, his eyes wide.

"Every time I see you, I just get sucked back in! Your face and—and your hair—ugh!" she groaned in frustration. "I need to burn the box!"

She tried to walk past him, but he put an arm out. "Wait a second," he pleaded. "What box? I'm completely lost! I said 'hi,' you got upset—what did I do wrong?"

Amanda's shoulders collapsed and she wiped her cheeks. "Evan, I'm going to tell you something, and I want you to promise not to make fun of me."

"Why would I—"

"Promise me! I have to get this out and be done with it."

"Okay, I promise," he said exasperated, dropping his arm and listening intently.

"I've become acutely aware over the last six months that I'm terrible at interpreting signals. And, I'm also apparently quite unaware of my own feelings sometimes, so that's...neat." She exhaled loudly, her cheeks flushing. "I don't think I ever got over...us," she said, swallowing hard. "I thought I did! I was engaged, I was honestly happy for you and—and—okay, that's a lie. I hated that you were dating Alexis, but I pretended I was happy for you two. That counts a little, right?" she said weakly, staring at the floor. "I really care about you, and I'm sorry I've been harboring this without even realizing it. It's not fair to you or me, and—"

"Can you stop for a second?" Evan said intensely, putting a hand under her chin and turning her splotchy face upward. "You're telling me that you have feelings for me still."

She nodded, "Good reflexive listening." Her face flushing an even deeper shade of red and she swallowed hard. "I mean, I did have feelings for you. Until I realized a few moments ago that you didn't feel the same way, and then I got really embarrassed and overwhelmed, and at least now it's out there—" Amanda stopped. Evan was holding his lips tightly together and his nostrils were flaring.

"Are you *laughing right now*?"

With her question, Evan couldn't hold it in any longer. A guffaw burst out of him, echoing off the walls and bouncing around in her ears.

"You promised you wouldn't make fun of me," she said, too emotionally off-center to hold back another round of tears.

"No!" he gasped, "This whole thing—" he motioned between them with his right hand, leaning on the counter for support with his left. "This is crazy!" he wheezed.

"I know!" Amanda shouted back at him, anger flaring within her. "It *is* crazy!" she shouted vehemently. "I don't know why I thought I could be vulnerable with you in the first place—you're the one who always talks about vulnerability!—and you can't even listen for two seconds—"

Before she knew what was happening, his lips were on hers. Desperate. Searching. Bewildered, she kissed him back before her brain was able to catch up. When it finally did, she pushed him away forcefully.

"You can't just kiss me and—suddenly make everything

—" she blustered, stopping short as her brain seemed to catch up again to the last few moments. Her eyes widened and she looked at him. His expression was serious, and his face flushed as he caught his breath.

"Are you—?" she started, and Evan continued to stare, a smile lifting the corners of his mouth. "This means—?"

Evan nodded. She darted forward, crushing her lips against his. She pressed her hands into his back, her whole body on fire. He felt perfect, and glorious, and—pushing back again, she looked him dead in the eyes.

"I'm serious, Evan. I'm done with the dating and the guessing games, and taking my time."

He nodded again, and ran his hands through her hair. "I know. I'm done with that, too." He pulled her to him, kissing her eyes, her jaw, her neck.

She leaned back, breathing hard. "Why didn't you tell me?"

"Tell you what?" he whispered.

"That you were leaving for Dubai?"

He relaxed his grip and took a deep breath. "I didn't know you cared. And I didn't—" he exhaled loudly. "I wasn't willing to bring it up out of the blue if I didn't have at least some idea that you were interested."

"I've been texting you all the time!" she argued.

"Yeah, but normal, friendly texts."

"What did you want me to say?" she asked, her eyes widening.

Evan threw back his head and laughed. "I don't know! I was being a coward, okay?" When she didn't respond, he continued, "I didn't sleep at all last night. I got home and was so turned around from traveling, I couldn't go to bed. So I worked all night. And felt sick in the morning, and yet all I wanted was to see you tonight. Even if I only got to watch you across the room, or see you laugh when Aarov did a stupid impression—"

"My impressions are never stupid!" Aarov called, and Evan whipped his head around. Amanda leaned to the left to see past him.

All seven of their friends stood huddled next to the wall with guilty smiles.

Leena smacked her husband. "They were just getting to the best part! You always open your big mouth—"

"How long have you been standing there?" Amanda asked, laughing nervously and wiping her eyes. When she looked up, she caught Alexis' eye and her heart squeezed. Alexis winked, and Amanda smiled half-heartedly.

"Shhh," Karl said. "Pretend we're not even here."

"Can we get a little privacy please?" Evan laughed, shooing them away.

The group reluctantly filtered back into the living room, leaving them alone.

Amanda cleared her throat. "Evan, what about Alexis—"

"We already talked over everything," he said.

Amanda blinked.

"Not *everything*," he clarified. "But when I knew I was coming tonight, I figured it was time for us to have a heart-to-heart. She's all in with Taylor. I think we're good."

Amanda sighed. "It's still probably going to be hard."

Evan nodded.

"So," she breathed, looping her arms around his neck. "You didn't sleep all night?"

"I slept all afternoon. So I could come and see you, remember?" he said softly, brushing his lips against hers.

"I'm glad you did."

"We're starting our game!" Karl yelled from the other room. "We're sick of waiting for you!"

Amanda laughed, lowering her arms and hugging him. "We can talk more later?"

"Mmhmm," he breathed. "First I have to school you at whatever weird game Nicole is making us play," he said, hurriedly picking up his food and dodging her as he rushed out of the room.

Amanda looked down at her plate on the counter. It held a lemon bar, hummus and vegetables, a mini quiche, and a mortifyingly tall mound of olives. Fitting. She picked it up and smiled to herself. Happy New Year, indeed.

## 13

## DECEMBER 31, 2013

"Hey," Amanda called down the hall, "Are you almost done? I was hoping you could—oh!"

Evan walked out of the bathroom with Toby wrapped in a soft cotton towel.

"You are done," Amanda cooed, smiling at her three-month-old as he kicked in delight.

"It's crazy how much he loves the water," Evan smiled. "I can barely get him washed because he wiggles around like crazy."

"I can't wait till he can sit up," Amanda said, walking back into the kitchen. "That'll be slightly easier."

She opened the fridge, and Evan leaned over to kiss her cheek.

"I'll go get him dressed in pj's," he said. "He can play on his mat for a bit until he gets tired. I can help you finish up with this."

"Thanks," Amanda said, pulling the avocados from the vegetable drawer. "We still have about thirty minutes before people will be showing up."

"Can you believe this is our first time hosting the New Year's Party?" Evan called down the hall.

"Took us long enough!" Amanda laughed, crushing a clove of garlic on the cutting board.

"YOUR HOME IS BEAUTIFUL!" LEENA SAID, HANGING UP HER coat. "I love everything you've done with it."

Amanda quickly showed off the new counters they'd had installed in the kitchen, and Leena helped her add ice to the water dispenser. They walked back into the living room and sat with the other women next to the piano.

"What's your next adventure?" Victoria was asking Alexis, and Amanda sat down to hear the answer.

"We're not totally sure," she said, "but Taylor's voting for a backpacking trip in eastern Europe. Timing will depend on when everything slows down for us after this fundraising season."

"You're keeping a list of all the places you go, right?" Nicole said. "Karl and I need to take some of these trips."

"The one problem with us working together is that we can't ever go together," Victoria said, nudging Nicole gently.

"We'll get another doctor in there eventually," Nicole smiled. "And then we need to *all* go on a trip."

"Somewhere warm," Leena said. "Without kids."

Amanda laughed but secretly couldn't imagine leaving Toby for more than a few hours. Maybe that would change when he was ten.

"Everyone!" Karl said, standing on the other side of the room. The women turned toward him. "I have something for you all, and I don't want to forget, so I'm going to give it to you now."

He walked over to the entry and slid a large bag carefully

across the floor, closer to the group. "Babe, can you help me with this?"

Nicole stood and walked over to him, allowing the bag and its contents to rest against her legs while he reached inside.

Karl pulled out a large, square picture frame and turned it toward the group. "Some of you know, my mom gave me Mike's old camera when he died. He had a goal of taking more photos in 2000, and obviously that never happened, so I was tasked with finishing off his film." He paused, collecting himself. "I've spent the last ten years taking a photo or two at our parties. I know Mike would've probably taken beautiful landscape shots, or pictures of incredible animals—he knew way more about this camera than I do," Karl laughed. "But, since this party was my way of remembering him, I decided this would be the perfect time to take those pictures."

He turned the frame around. "I have one of these for each of you. They're all different. I picked photos I thought you'd like, and if you don't, you can always look at the negatives and choose something different. This one's for Leena and Aarov."

He walked over and handed it to Leena, and she motioned for Aarov to sit next to her.

"Victoria and Jesse," Karl said, pulling out the next frame and delivering it.

"Alexis and Taylor," he said, and Alexis stood to take it from him.

"And last but not least, Evan and Amanda."

Amanda motioned for Evan to take it, and he brought it over to her. She slid from her chair onto the floor so she could get a closer look.

"Look at this," she said softly.

"That's the night you apologized to me," Evan said.

"Which time?" Amanda laughed.

"The first time, after we didn't see each other that whole year. Remember?"

"How do you know it was that night?"

"Because I remember what you were wearing."

Amanda smiled. "Sledding," she said, pointing to a picture of Evan covered in snow. "That was an amazing night."

"Ooh, this was when we were at the Marriott," Evan said, and Amanda cocked her head to the side.

"Were you looking at me? That's me, right? That's my hair."

Evan nodded, and she turned to look at him. "You were checking me out."

"Maybe," Evan said, turning back to the frame. "What's this one?"

Amanda followed his finger and her breath caught in her throat. Her hair was shorter, and she had her old hiking backpack.

"Mike took this," she breathed. "We went hiking. This was at the top while we were eating our lunches. I had no idea..." She traced along the glass with her fingertip, remembering that day.

"Did I ever tell you that Mike mentioned you to me? Before we met?"

Amanda shook her head, intrigued.

"He came home one night—I think you'd been skiing for the first time?"

"Mmmhmm."

"He was completely amped up. Couldn't even shower before telling me about it. I remember because everything he said about you—it was like you were the most amazing person he'd ever met."

Tears began to collect in the corners of her eyes.

"And then the first time I saw you," he continued, "was lying in a hospital bed. I couldn't even see your face. But I knew Mike thought you were the coolest person ever. That's why I stayed."

"You told me it was because Deb wanted you to," she laughed, as a tear rolled down her cheek.

"And that was true," Evan nodded. "She was really upset about it. But, I'd be lying if I didn't say his description intrigued me. I think that's why I never told you," he said, looking back at the frame. "I was kind of embarrassed that after losing him, there was a small part of me that was still only thinking of myself."

Amanda set the frame against the wall and hugged him, laying her cheek against his chest. "You're not giving yourself enough credit," she said softly. "But I'm glad you stayed. And I'm glad you're mine."

*"What are you thinking about?" Amanda asked, following Mike's gaze over the lake.*

*"How grateful I am to be alive right now."*

*"In 1999?"*

*Mike laughed. "No. Right now, with you. On this beautiful mountain top."*

*She set down her sandwich and looked at him. "How do you do that?"*

*"What?"*

*"Take in each moment so completely. It's like you're never worried about what comes next."*

*Mike shrugged. "I guess I'm not."*

*"But how? My brain keeps moving forward, wondering what I need to study or what I'm going to do when I graduate. You know? You're sitting there thinking that, and I'm sitting here thinking...I might need to buy more bread at the grocery store."*

*Mike threw back his head and laughed. "Here," he said, setting down his pack and walking over to her. "I'll show you."*

*He sat next to her on the cold rock, avoiding the patches of snow. "Look," he said, pointing up to a mountain jay sitting on the branch of a pine tree to their left. "Isn't it beautiful?"*

*Amanda nodded.*

*"I like to watch it and just notice its movements. And look at this," he said pointing to the base of the tree. "Do you see that little tree poking out of the snow?"*

*Amanda nodded again.*

*"Think how long that's been growing to only get that tall. And see how the needles are slightly different colors? Trees are so cool. And down there in the water, see how it's all different colors depending on the depth?"*

*She did see, and she smiled.*

*Mike sighed, leaning back on his hands. "You can't really worry about bread when you're watching all of that."*

*"No," Amanda laughed, "I guess not." She took another bite of her sandwich and wrapped the rest up, putting it back in her pack. "So that's the key? Noticing things?"*

*"You can't be unhappy when you're noticing beautiful things. It's impossible." He smiled, standing back up. "I'm going to find a spot to go to the bathroom. Head back down in five or so?"*

*"Sounds great," Amanda said, turning back to the lake.*

*She noticed the way the branch in front of her bounced when a small sparrow jumped off of it and flew to another tree. She noticed how the air smelled crisp and fresh as she breathed it into her lungs. She noticed the way the snow melted and left lacy edges of ice along the drifts.*

*She smiled and sighed contentedly. It was beautiful. It was all so beautiful.*

THE END

## ALSO BY CINDY GUNDERSON

Tier Trilogy (Tier 1, Tier 2, Tier 3)

I Can't Remember

Let's Try This Again, But This Time in Paris

Yes, And

Holly Bough Cottage

www.CindyGunderson.com

Instagram: @CindyGWrites

Facebook: @CindyGWrites

# ABOUT THE AUTHOR

Cindy is first and foremost mother to her four beautiful children and wife to her charming and handsome husband, Scott. She is a musician, a homeschooler, a gardener, an athlete, an actor, a lover of Canadian chocolate, and most recently, a writer.

Cindy grew up in Airdrie, AB, Canada, but has lived most of her adult life between California and Colorado. She currently resides in the Denver metro area. Cindy graduated from Brigham Young University in 2005 with a B.S. in Psychology, minoring in Business. She serves actively within her church and community and is always up for a new adventure.

f 🄾